A Candlelight Ecstasy Romance®

"I LEFT YOUR KIND OF LIFE BEHIND," SAL EXPLAINED.

"I like you, but I can see that even a fling or a summer affair with you would be all-consuming. I don't need—or want—that sort of intensity in my life."

"You can really be that objective?" Robert inquired.

"You like to dominate . . . everything." Sal's soft smile took the sting out of her words. "Business, of course, *and* your relationships."

A smile flickered on Robert's mouth. "I have two ex-wives, and they both accused me of the same thing. Why is it that hearing it from you doesn't make me angry or defensive?"

"Because I'm not your wife." Sal laughed for the first time since he'd arrived.

"Marry me and you will be."

CANDLELIGHT ECSTASY ROMANCES®

SHENANDOAH SUMMER

Samantha Hughes

A CANDLELIGHT ECSTASY ROMANCE®

Published by
Dell Publishing Co., Inc.
1 Dag Hammarskjold Plaza
New York, New York 10017

Dell ® TM 681510, Dell Publishing Co., Inc.

Candlelight Ecstasy Romance®, 1,203,540, is a registered
trademark of Dell Publishing Co., Inc., New York, New York.

ISBN: 0-440-18045-7

Printed in the United States of America

First printing—January 1985

To Our Readers:

We have been delighted with your enthusiastic response to Candlelight Ecstasy Romances®, and we thank you for the interest you have shown in this exciting series.

In the upcoming months we will continue to present the distinctive, sensuous love stories you have come to expect only from Ecstasy. We look forward to bringing you many more books from your favorite authors and also the very finest work from new authors of contemporary romantic fiction.

As always, we are striving to present the unique, absorbing love stories that you enjoy most—books that are more than ordinary romance. Your suggestions and comments are always welcome. Please write to us at the address below.

Sincerely,

The Editors
Candlelight Romances
1 Dag Hammarskjold Plaza
New York, New York 10017

CHAPTER ONE

A faint smile formed on Sal Carter's strong-boned face as she rolled onto her back and brushed a damp wisp of thick blond hair off her smooth tanned forehead. Since moving into the crumbling old antebellum mansion located in the heart of Virginia she'd made only two concessions to civilized living. She'd bought a king-size bed with an extra-firm mattress to accommodate her curvaceous five feet eleven inch body; and she'd purchased a fancy electrical French coffeemaker with a timer set to go off at five o'clock every morning, thus ensuring that the hearty aroma of her favorite blend of Colombian coffee would waft through the house. It was more effective than an alarm clock.

Sal flung one long muscular arm off the bed and savored the rich aroma with her eyes closed. Coffee was one vice she could never imagine giving up. With or without coffee she had always been a bundle of nervous energy. And she'd observed, with that uncanny acumen she had for mathematical details and statistics, that most people developed a problem with caffeine in their forties. So since she had just turned thirty, she still had another ten years to indulge.

She opened her eyes slowly, the smile broadening as she considered the absurdity of her early-morning meandering thoughts. How she loved waking up alone in the rambling old house with the hush of the humid dawn hanging in the air like the filmy cobwebs that clung in the corners of the high ceilings.

With the summer heat in full bloom, these few moments of suspended time were especially rare, for only between the early-morning hours of four thirty and six thirty was there any respite from the heat. By eight, when she finished milking the cows and headed out to gather the eggs (if there were any in this heat) she would be perspiring. By ten thirty, when she completed her chores and returned to the kitchen to polish off the remaining coffee, the thermometer would be inching toward one hundred. She didn't even want to think about the humidity!

Sal put her slender feet on the hardwood floor next to the bed and stared at her toes. Had she once really worn nail polish on her toes? She wriggled her toes and chuckled at the image of her former self: the sleekly coiffured young advertising executive who dressed in the latest fashions, sipped dry martinis with absolutely no side effects, and managed to close more deals during her first year of employment than most executives hoped to close in five. Maybe it had been too damn easy. To this day she wasn't sure if she'd been driven out of the business world because it was too hard or too easy.

It had certainly been easy enough to succeed, she thought, if that was what you wanted to call it. That's what everyone in the advertising business in Chicago had called it. Success! Sally Evans Carter, creative wizard, an overnight success at twenty-four. Clients had swarmed to her like wasps to a pool of water in August. And really, when she thought of it now, she'd been no more creative than most of her colleagues, and she'd been a good deal less ambitious than some of them. Her success, she mused, had been entirely the result of her strapping, healthy appearance, her soft drawling Virginia accent, and her unflagging ability to call a spade a spade. Actually, some people might have seen the latter as a handicap. Bluntness was what it really was, and if she had stuck it out, her candid nature would have inevitably netted her a thorny reputation.

Not that she made light of her accomplishments. She knew they were considerable, and however much luck had been involved in opening her own advertising agency when she was only twenty-six years old, she was at heart thankful for the opportunity. As a student at the University of Virginia, she had never dreamed of making the kind of money she'd made. A college roommate and chance had taken her west to Chicago, and she had fallen into a job at a small advertising agency. The rest, as she thought of it now, had just *happened*. She had skyrocketed to the top of the advertising heap like the heroine of a movie with fast cuts and little narrative. After her first very successful advertising campaign with Allen & Newberg, she was awarded two accounts of her own, and when those two campaigns took off, she was made a vice-president. Five years later, when Allen and Newberg parted company, one of their major clients offered to underwrite her in her own agency.

Sal sighed. Ah, youth! She padded into the bathroom, stripped off the oversize white T-shirt she wore as a nightie, and wound her shoulder-length hair into a knot before stepping under a cool shower. It still amazed her that she had never taken any of that Chicago fairy tale seriously. None of it had seemed real, even while it had been happening. And now that she was back in Virginia, a bona fide farmer who spent four or five hours at her easel every day, her nine years in Chicago seemed dim—like a late movie that one recalls vaguely the following morning.

Had she really founded her own advertising agency, seen it flourish for three fast-paced years, and then, without blinking an eye, sold all but five percent of her interest in the business? She could count on one hand the people who didn't think she was crazy for giving all that up! Actually, she could count them on one finger—Abe Frankenworth, a fellow artist and her closest friend since college, was the only person she knew who really understood.

She doubted if her family would ever understand why she would want to come back to Albemarle County, Virginia, and camp out in a dilapidated, unfurnished eighteen-room house that she was leasing from an absentee landlord, along with the barns and twenty of the five hundred acres of land. Farmers themselves, her folks had little to show for their years of hard work and couldn't understand why their daughter, who had proved she could be successful in the business world, wanted to be a farmer too.

"A farm?" Her father had patted the sparse white hair on his head and looked dumbfounded when Sal told him her plan. "Alone? Just you? No one else?"

Yes, just her alone. No one else except, of course, Abe, who lived in little room in nearby Charlottesville and used two of the eighteen rooms in the farmhouse for his studio. Occasionally when he worked late, he slept over on an old cot they'd scavenged from the

Charlottesville dump. But most of the time she was alone.

"Alone? No telephone? Sally, be sensible, you've got to have a phone!" Her mother, not an unreasonable woman, had been appalled. "A woman alone in the middle of nowhere . . . twenty minutes from Charlottesville? No, you can't count Blue Mills. Blue Mills can hardly be called a town. They don't even have a post office."

"They've got a good bar." Sal had winked at her dad, but Andrew Carter had only slumped farther down in his easy chair, lamenting the fate of his favorite child. He had been so sure she'd given up all her notions of being an artist. Of all his eight children he'd been certain that Sally would amount to something. And now she was going to be a farming artist without a phone.

"At least put in a telephone, Sal. What's got into you? You always had good sense till now."

"They'll be phoning me from Chicago," she had tried to explain to her mother. "Nobody there's taking me seriously. They think it's a whim. They're sure they can lure me back, and I know they'll be calling for advice."

So she moved in without a phone. And she lived alone, feeling absolutely terrified. For the entire month of March she had jumped and twitched at every noise, bolted the doors and windows, and slept with the lights on. Not even Abe knew that her first month had been a battle against horrible imaginings. She had pleaded insomnia and staggered through spring planting like a zombie, more determined than ever not to install a phone.

She'd read Emerson and Thoreau and spent her waking hours thinking about self-reliance. What did it mean to be self-sufficient? She had always thought she was. Certainly she had never been frightened living alone in her Lake Shore apartment in Chicago. What was there on the farm that scared her so? She was Sal Carter—Tall Sal they had called her in school. She had always been athletic, could still swim two miles without much effort and, though she seldom played tennis anymore, her backhand was as wicked as ever. So what was she so afraid of?

It was nearly the end of April when she finally realized what lay at the root of her fear, and then her discovery came quite by accident. One night Abe had stayed in his studio quite late and she had peeked in and found him curled up, snoring in one corner. She threw a blanket over him and returned to her own bed, immediately falling into a blissful sleep.

There had been a man in the house! And the next morning she had her answer—though it made her cringe inside to admit it. She had slept peacefully because Abe's presence had made her feel protected. She blanched at the absurdity of her thinking. Abe Frankenworth would be about as much protection against an intruder as a toy poodle. All six feet of him was bones, he was usually out of breath from too many cigarettes, and she doubted if he'd exercised since he was seven! Yet Abe's presence had sent her happily off to dreamland. She'd debated about buying a dog, but stubbornly decided to stick it out alone. That night she fell asleep, woke around two, and checked the front door. She then fell back asleep, without Abe's presence under her roof.

Now she was used to living here alone. Sal bounded down the creaky curved staircase and went into the kitchen to pour herself a cup of coffee. Since she'd overcome her insidious fear, she felt a greater sense of accomplishment than she had felt over any of her smoothly executed deals in the big time.

A farmer at heart, Sal gulped down her coffee, rolled the bottoms of her Levi's overalls up to her knees, and headed for the sagging red barn. Too bad she didn't have enough money to buy this piece of property, she thought, and to restore the house and the outbuildings to their former beauty.

Tara Junior, as she and Abe had christened the place, had been purchased as an investment, like many of the large tracts of land in Albemarle County, by a financial mogul who had probably never even seen the Shenandoah Valley. There was a precedent for rich and powerful people buying up the countryside in and around Charlottesville. Ever since Thomas Jefferson extolled the virtues of the rolling Virginia land and built Monticello, the Shenandoah Valley was known as prime property. But unlike some of the current land owners, Sal mused, Jefferson's commitment to the land went beyond money, as had James Monroe's, whose five-hundred-fifty-acre estate was only fifteen minutes away. But both Monroe and Jefferson had lived here. Jefferson's idea of profit, thought Sal as she waved to one of the high school students who helped her with chores, was more than economics. For men like Jefferson and Monroe there was also profit of the spirit. The beauty of the green rolling countryside could not be measured merely in dollars and cents, as it was now being done by the absentee landlords.

"Hey, Wendell . . ." Sal loped over to a tall, gangling blond boy. "Check the heifers down in the lower pasture. I think that trough's dried up down there, and you may want to herd them back farther to the stream."

"Yes, ma'am." The sixteen-year-old saluted Sal shyly and averted his eyes from her shapely calves.

"Going to be another scorcher." Sal leaned against the flaking white fence and gazed off to the west, marveling at the distinctly bluish range of mountains. Wendell Savitz and his buddy Munson Jones both had crushes on her, a detail which made her role as employer a trifle uncomfortable.

"Dry . . ." Sal bent down and scooped up a handful of dirt. "Rain yesterday didn't do a thing."

"Supposed to rain again today." Wendell shifted uneasily away from her.

"Well, if it doesn't"—Sal straightened up and headed for the chicken coop—"you and Munson take off this afternoon. Go swimming—or doze under a tree. It's too hot to do anything else. I mean it. Knock off by noon and skedaddle!"

"Yes, ma'am!" Wendell called after her as she disappeared into the hen house.

Six eggs. At this rate she was not exactly going to make a fortune in her first year on the farm. Sal chuckled to herself and trooped into the barn. There, she sat on an old red trunk, mending a halter for one of the very costly Hereford bulls she'd invested in. Her blond hair loosened from its off-center knot, and her cheeks were flushed.

She had to expect a deficit for at least five years, she told herself. The main thing was to keep the deficit down until she could build her herd and perfect some of her farming skills. Of course, it wasn't profitable to plant on a small scale, but she'd indulged, just this once, in the idea of the old traditional truck garden, and planted a little bit of everything. It gave her a sense of satisfaction to see her produce—the plump tomatoes, bright carrots, bunches of scallions, beans, and eggplant lined up in the little vegetable stand at the foot of her driveway. She liked selling eggs and milk to the local Blue Mills general store. But she chided herself that once she found a farm she could afford to buy with the

16

money from the ad agency, she would not be able to indulge in romantic ideas about farming.

Several hours later, having completed her round of chores, she sat on the back porch sipping what was left of her morning coffee. Somehow the scalding stuff cooled her down. The sad thing about an absentee landlord was that the old home she was living in was rotting away. But there was no way, Sal had decided, she was going to put a penny of her own money into restoring a house that someone else owned. She'd already had to shell out five hundred dollars to mend some fences so her bulls wouldn't wander off. That had been a necessity. Mending the roof was a different story. She just put buckets under the leaks and moved her bed to another room. Of course, she'd notified the real estate agent who rented her the place, but that had been months ago. So far, she thought, there was no sign that the great mogul gave a damn about his leaky roof.

Sal frowned and wiped the sweat off her forehead as Abe's battered VW bumped into sight.

"Hi, honey." She waved lethargically—like a southern belle, she thought wryly. "Heat got you down? You're late."

Abe's dark hair was a tight mass of ringlets. He was beaming as he approached her, carrying a large carton. "Two fans." He set the box down on the porch. "I don't know how you can sleep without a fan, Sal."

"You didn't buy—Abe, you can't afford to go buyin' me fans."

"The least I can do, m'lady." Abe gave a deep bow and kissed her hand like a gallant southern gentleman.

Sal gave a low chuckle. "Somethin' in this heat and cloyin' humidity is makin' us both behave like southern aristocrats. I was just sittin' here thinkin'. For the first time since I arrived here, I could use a little pamperin'.

17

Look at me. . . ." Sal stretched out her tanned legs. Her feet were barely encased in holey sneakers, there was a rip in the pocket of her overalls, and the red bandanna scarf at her neck was faded a pale pink.

Abe removed a pair of glasses from his pocket, put them on, and peered closely at her. "You look beautiful. Like you're posing for *Farm Vogue*. Maybe it's the newest trend. I mean, what can come after punk?"

Sal gave a robust laugh. "The hayseed look! Boy, I got it, Abe, and so do you. I want you to take a picture of me and I'll send it to my friends in Chicago. They still don't believe I'm doin' it with my own two hands."

She turned her large hands over and stared at her grubby palms with a dismayed look. "Do you think I've gone overboard, Abe? Look at these calluses."

Abe nudged her playfully as he went into the house. "I think you need a little action, girl. And I don't mean with your easel. Dorie says there's a new physics professor who's—"

"I know, I know," Sal interrupted with a grin. "Six feet six, handsome and witty. Why is the main criteria for fixing me up always the man's height?"

"Because"—Abe stuck his head back outside the screen door—"short guys aren't interested in you, Sal."

"All of a sudden," Sal lamented, half seriously, "there's a dearth of tall men. Chicago was full of them. Tall, *dull* men. I started to develop a theory that all the really intriguing, nice, fascinating, brilliant, sexy men are short. Look at Brando, Pacino, De Niro, and even Robert Redford isn't that tall."

"I'm tall," teased Abe, "and I'm fascinating and sexy."

"And so is Dorie." Sal flashed him a smile over her shoulder. "Okay, I'll meet whatsisname. As long as he doesn't stay out late. From now on *my* main criteria for

18

male companionship will be whether or not he's an early to bed, early to riser."

"Sounds exciting." Abe gave her a dubious look.

After Abe retreated upstairs to his studio Sal went inside, gathered up her painting equipment, and headed down across the meadow toward the woods at the rear of the property. Technically, she wasn't leasing the woods, just twenty acres of farm and pasture land. But as soon as the crops were sown, she had spent afternoons hiking all over the property. In her travels she had discovered one particularly lush area where a meandering rocky stream led to a tiny but fierce cascading waterfall, forming a deep green pool at its base.

Since June she had spent almost every afternoon in the secluded spot, working on a series of medium-size oil paintings in a variety of styles. Now, for the first time, she felt she knew where her passion for painting would lead her. At heart she was not an abstract artist. She had known that, but in an attempt to remain objective and explore as many styles of painting as possible, she had rendered two canvases in her own interpretation of abstract expressionism.

At heart she was a realist. Sal hummed an old Beatles melody under her breath as she set up her portable easel and squeezed out a few colors of paint onto her palette. She painted what she saw, focusing on the details of this tropical paradise. After all, she thought, it was her talent for calling a spade a spade that had catapulted her to financial success in the advertising business. And so she would paint that way.

She looked up into the leafy bower, the green so thick there was scarcely a hint of blue in that one area directly above her head. Her heart was pounding, her brown eyes widened with an intensity that few who knew her had ever seen. She tilted her head to one side, altering the perspective slightly. Yes, she would paint precisely what she saw—a canvas bursting with verdant hues. So many shades of green, from a silvery pale to a rich fecund black, and if she was successful there would be a sense of movement, too, as if those shifting slivers of blue sky were about to leap out from behind the pulsating green!

"Hey diddle diddle, the cat and the fiddle!" Four and a half hours later she returned to the house, singing. There was an exhausted dreamy smile on her face as she lugged her work upstairs to one of the many rooms designated as studios. She pressed her ear to Abe's door, but the silence told her he was hard at work, so she didn't disturb him. How she wished she could return to that sacred spot and paint at night. Well, perhaps she could, she thought—some night when the moon was full, with its light reflecting off the water. Now that she had seized upon a way of painting that was truly hers, her mind was on fire with ideas. She would paint hundreds of pictures of that spot—in all seasons.

"Hey diddle diddle," she sang in a throaty voice as she plugged in the coffee maker. It hadn't rained yet, though she'd heard distant thunder. She decided she'd go out to the front pasture along the lane and check the two young cows due to give birth soon. She went into the small lavatory off the kitchen, splashed some cold water on her face, and rewound her hair into a tighter knot to get it off her neck. It was nearly five thirty and not a sign of a break in the heat. It took your appetite away, Sal thought. It would do her good to lose a pound or two, and since the only time she could diet was when she didn't want to eat, she'd consider this heat wave a summer diet and be thankful. She smiled, patting her well-rounded hips as she slammed the screen door.

"How you doin'?" Sal threaded her way among the

white-faced Herefords, patting their heads, stroking the slender horns of those who had horns. Cows were her favorite animal.

She knew that even if she were to become one of the lucky few who could earn a living solely by painting, she would still want to farm. There was something about being surrounded by living creatures, and the garden, too, that gave her an expansiveness, a peacefulness she had missed during her years in the city. Even though her funds were quickly dwindling, Sal was happier now than she had ever been in her life.

She plunked herself down in the midst of the cattle, pulled a long strand of grass and sucked on it as she stared at the Shenandoah Mountains. The hue had deepened since early morning and there were a few dark clouds hovering along the southern tips. A good soaking was what they needed, she thought, one of the sudden violent storms that rips out the electrical power and shakes the house. Now, even the idea of being plunged into total darkness held no fear for her. It was funny, she mused, how things changed. Sometimes suddenly the thing that most frightened you became the thing you loved most.

She stretched out on her back, so engrossed in her thoughts that she did not hear the black Porsche that inched slowly up the lane. Nor did she hear the car door slam, or feel the presence of the man who walked over to the fence and stood staring out at the spectacle of the beautiful young blonde sprawled lazily among the grazing cattle.

The stranger stood for a while, a perplexed, quizzical expression on his handsome face. He was dark, and in his finely cut suit with a proper tie knotted at his neck, he looked alarmingly out of place. He folded his hands on the top of the fence, noting that the paint was peeling. His profile was sharp and arresting, his dark eyes burning with a constant intensity whether he was regarding the flaking paint or the woman in the field. He glanced at his watch with the same impatient intensity.

Judging from the few gray hairs at the temples of his sleek black hair, he was perhaps in his early forties, though the boiling intensity of his disposition may have contributed more to the finely etched lines in his face and the tautness of his jaw and jutting chin than his actual age. Beneath his raw silk suit his body seemed restless, wired for the next endeavor. He looked at his watch a second time, turned back to the car, then thought better of it and returned to the fence to stare again at Sal Carter, whose long languid posture had not changed. He opened his mouth to speak, then stopped as his gaze cooled and an unwelcome thought seemed to shatter the sophisticated composure of his face. He stared harder, craning his neck to one side to get a better look at her. His shiny brown shoe inched toward the bottom rung of the fence as if he were about to climb up to have still a better view of her. Then suddenly he frowned, shook himself, and called out in a deep voice that was accustomed to shouting orders.

"I say, this is the Capolla property, isn't it? I'm looking for an S. Carter. Just wanted to make sure this was the right place."

Sal bolted to her feet, her heart racing, her throat constricted. It wasn't just that she was startled by the unexpected appearance of a stranger. No, it was the timbre of his deep voice. It left her feeling unsettled, endangered.

She stared over the cattle and met his dark eyes, even more acutely aware of how extremely casual she had grown in her appearance. The overalls, though baggy in the seat, were cut low around the arms, and she was

22

more aware than she would have liked of her ample breasts, of the voluptuousness of her tanned body as she moved toward him. She swallowed hard, smiled, and waited for her steadiness to take control. "May I help you?" She eyed him narrowly. He wasn't from around here. Probably Washington, she thought, or some other fast-paced metropolis.

"Well, that's a good question." He laughed at her polite inquiry. She stiffened at the thinly disguised suggestiveness.

"Yes . . . well." He drew his admiring eyes away from her and adopted a more businesslike attitude. "Maybe you can help me locate the S. Carter who rents this place."

"I'm sure I can." Sal regarded him evenly. She didn't like the way he was making her feel, so uneasy and so nervous. She drew herself up to her full height, enjoying his momentary confusion. So he was looking for S. Carter, was he? And who did he think she was?

"Do you know where he is?" His eyes flashed with a touch of well-practiced impatience.

Sal grinned suddenly. Why was she taking this so seriously? Just because he'd interrupted her reverie, made a flirtatious innuendo? Still, she found it hard to resist shattering that cool, sophisticated, self-important businessman's air.

"I'm S. Carter," she confirmed with a precise bob of her blond head.

"Well, I'll be damned!"

His unaffected response took her by surprise. Not at all the rigid, controlled response of the highly polished corporate executive she judged him to be. Her eyes matched his smiling ones as she stretched out her hand.

"I'll be damned," he repeated as he clasped her rough, paint-splotched hand in his smooth, perfectly

23

manicured one. His grip was warm and firm, and he continued holding it as he regarded her.

"Sorry." Sal removed her hand. "I couldn't resist baiting you a bit. You had no way of knowing S. Carter was a woman."

"I guess not." He chuckled, then looked at her again with his piercing black eyes.

She moved away from him and stood with her back against a fence post. She still wasn't feeling in control. The touch of his warm flesh on her hand had fused her with a tingling uneasiness. Realizing she hadn't seen a man in a business suit since she'd left Chicago, she thought maybe that was what was throwing her.

"I don't know any Capolla," she said calmly.

He was watching her intently, as if she were some strange novelty. "This is the Capolla property. Is this where you live?"

"It certainly is," Sal confirmed with a smile. "These are my cattle, my garden is over there, my stand down at the foot of the lane."

"And Harry O'Brien down at Blue Mills Realty rented you this place?" He tried to adopt a professional tone but the bewildered expression did not entirely leave his face. Well, she guessed, she probably was some kind of novelty to him.

After all, not everyone was used to the *Farm Vogue* look.

"That's right," she confirmed. "People around here call him Gabby. I mean they call him that to his face, since he calls himself that. I'm surprised he didn't tell you S. Carter was a woman. I get the impression he thinks I'm a little daft for livin' up here."

She volunteered the information in a voice that was not quite her own. How did he manage to look so cool? He nodded slowly and looked out toward the range of mountains. For a moment Sal stared at him, her long tanned arms hanging loosely at her sides, her brown eyes questioning. There was something disturbing about his sudden appearance, yet she could not bring herself to even consider the reasons for his being here.

He turned his dark eyes toward her suddenly and the cataclysmic effect of their penetrating intensity caught her completely off-guard. She looked away instantly, but her breath continued to quiver in her throat, and there was a deep, erotic stillness between them, something tight and pent-up, just like the air feels before a storm.

"Low pressure system." Sal rationalized the unsettling feeling out loud. "It storms nearly every afternoon but never enough to do any real good.

"Like I said," she went on firmly, taking herself in hand with her usual straightforward efficiency, "I am S. Carter, Sal to be exact, and I'm the tenant farmer here. Gabby rented me the place. He handles the leases for a lot of the absentee landlords around here. I'm sure he could answer any of your questions about the property."

"There was a gone fishin' sign on his door." He grinned, shaking his head. "I never saw a gone fishin' sign before. I thought they were bogus, like the proverbial unicorn."

Sal smiled at his analogy. Her first impression of him as a cut-from-the-mold, three-piece-suit businessman whose mind worked with the brutal, humorless efficiency of a computer, was quickly being dispelled.

"Gabby goes fishin' every day." She laughed. "Sometimes twice a day. I'd guess you'd have to say that if you rated the eccentric characters in Blue Mills, Gabby would come out pretty close to the top of the list. Understand, I'm not disparaging his skills as a real estate agent. He has his own style. People like doin' business with him . . . even the big corporations. Well, you probably know that most of these large tracts of land down here have been gobbled up by big corporations. Gabby may have mentioned which corporation owns this spread but to be honest with you, I disregarded it. Anyhow, I'm sure it wasn't Capolla."

"And you don't like the idea of corporations gobbling up all this bucolic wonder?"

It was a subject on which she had been known to wax eloquent, a subject which could rouse her ire more quickly than any other. "I'm going to tell you what I think"—she met his eyes warily—"and then you're going to tell me you're the lawyer representing such and such a corporation."

"Maybe." He raised a challenging eyebrow. "Would that stop you from speaking your mind?"

"Maybe," Sal chuckled, and thrust her hands deeper into her pockets in an effort to dispel the quivering sensations that still fluttered through her body. She liked him but she didn't want to like him. She knew his type, she thought.

"You don't like lawyers either." He took a step forward, as if he sensed her reaction to his charismatic virility.

Damn him! She knew what kind of man he was: smart, clever, witty, capable of playing a variety of games, and on top of it all, ambitious.

"I don't lump people into categories," Sal replied with a smile.

He gave her a tight smile, as if he didn't believe her.

"All right." She felt a strange, unfettered excitement as she began. "I'll tell you how I feel and then we'll see if I've insulted you or not. Here is Sal Carter on Absentee Landlords. Briefly."

"Make it as long as you like." He fastened his dark eyes on her and listened with a fascinated expression.

"As you know, Albemarle County has some of the richest farmland in the country, one of the few areas in the East where there are still huge, unspoiled tracts of land. There's a sense of history here. Jefferson and Monroe, to name only two, elected to settle here, and with good reason. It was near enough to where the action was, and far enough removed to afford true solitude. It still is. The pity is that these modern-day absentee landlords are totally disconnected from everything that goes on here. Most of them have never even seen their properties. They rent out beautiful old antebellum mansions for a song, but so what? Most of the houses are crumbling to the ground. Nobody who pays five hundred dollars a month rent can afford the upkeep on these places. They rent off farmland in a haphazard way that suits *their* economics but has nothing to do with the economics of the area. It's all tax write-offs, deductions. The potential of the community is the last consideration. Well, the most obvious result is that they've driven the costs of the land up so high that locals can't afford to buy here anymore. How can young couples starting out compete with multi-million dollar corporations?" Sal broke off abruptly, flushed from her impassioned monologue.

"Are you a politician?" he asked her seriously.

"Not on your life." Sal dug in her pocket and mopped her brow with a tissue. "Maybe I spend too much time here by myself." She smiled ruefully, avoiding his inquisitive gaze. "I'm a farmer. Like I said . . . I rent all this."

"But not alone. . . ." he stated tentatively, as if he hoped it wasn't true.

"Indeed alone." Sal felt suddenly unnerved at having

27

revealed so much. "Okay, now who are you? I'm prepared for the worst."

"You're sure?" he asked, teasing.

Sal raised her eyes slowly and met his gaze, knowing that the slightest connection would unleash those unwanted flutterings. Abe was right. She had been ignoring one whole, very large portion of her life.

"I'll wager you already know the answer." He put one shiny shoe on the lower rung of the old fence.

So he liked games. Sal scanned his handsome face. He had to be a lawyer. He was young, smart, and cagey.

"I have several properties in the vicinity." He held her eyes.

The faintness she felt in the pit of her stomach was not the result of his words. She lowered her eyes, then looked back at him directly. "So . . . I've insulted you, after all."

"Intrigued," he corrected her with an unmistakably flirtatious glance. "Not insulted. Intrigued. I am Robert Capolla . . . your absentee landlord."

28

CHAPTER TWO

Sal regained her poise instantly. "Well, we both took a risk, didn't we? I risked insulting you and you risked being insulted." Actually, she had taken much of the sting out of her little speech, just in case. . . .

Robert Capolla's eyes took in her sultry dishevelment, which was the result of a long hard day. "I should guess that you are not unaccustomed to taking risks. You seemed to approach it all with a good deal of relish."

"I guess you're right." Sal gave a low, throaty laugh and looked away. But when she looked back at him, he was grinning, and suddenly they were both standing with their backs against the peeling fence, laughing.

"You're not going to ask me to leave, are you?" Sal broke off in a sudden panic.

"Not anymore." Robert's eyes caressed her.

"What do you mean, not anymore? Is that why you came here? You can't just go around breaking leases.

Well, maybe you can. I mean, I couldn't afford to go to court if you—"

"Hey!" He reached out and touched her bare arm, making her flesh tingle. "I'm not going to evict you. I am not the villain in the piece."

"What piece?" Sal tensed, so as not to shiver from the delicious sensation of his fingers, which were still clasped lightly on her upper arm.

"This little pastoral scenario we're playing out here," he explained. "That's what piece."

He withdrew his hand circumspectly, and they stood for a moment in silence.

"Funny," he said after a moment. "I imagined S. Carter to be some husky young man with a wife and six little kids. I imagined trikes in the front yard, a tire hanging from the tree. Harry O'Brien—I mean Gabby —just sent my attorney a copy of the lease with the signature *S. Carter* on it. I never even saw the contract. I just called my attorney before I left New York to get the name."

"I see," Sal replied levelly.

Robert's dark eyes twinkled. "Did you curse me for the faulty plumbing?"

Sal laughed. "Several times . . . a week!"

"That bad?"

"Worse!" Sal felt a wild rush of energy coursing through her body.

When Robert Capolla laughed, his handsome angular face, almost stern when in repose, was utterly transformed. It was as if two men existed inside one form. The laughing Robert possessed the same dark, intriguing charisma, but with an added sensitivity that was altogether absent from the stern Robert. Sal kept sneaking looks, enthralled by the extreme contrast. The laughing Robert was years younger, impulsive, unpredictable. The solemn Robert was a driven man, a calculator hell-bent on driving home the best deal. Sal knew all about the solemn Robert. She had done business with men like that, had even been expeditiously courted by a few of them.

"Since you didn't come down here to ask me to leave," she said, eyeing the darkening horizon, "why don't you come on up to the house and I'll give you a cup of coffee?"

"Why are you here?" Robert asked her with the same intrigued look on his face.

"What do you mean, why am I here?" Sal felt the irrepressible excitement bubble in her throat.

"You're not really a farmer." He gave her such an appealing look that her heart lurched in response.

"I am!" she affirmed. "But I'm an artist too. Let's talk in the house. We'll get caught in a downpour if we don't get a move on."

"I'll give you a lift." Robert reached for her hand to help her over the fence, but Sal was already moving toward the gate.

"No, you drive on," she called over her shoulder as she broke into a slow trot. "I have to check the chickens."

Check the chickens, indeed, she thought. She had to do no such thing. She had to get away from this man for a moment, that was what she had to do. She felt the perspiration popping out as she trotted toward the chicken coop. Good Lord, she would expire from a heart attack if she didn't slow down. Only Sal didn't slow down: Running made her less aware of the palpitations zinging through her body, the heady excitement that had overtaken her during the conversation with Robert Capolla. She ran faster, feeling her heart pound with a steady, hard rhythm which was comforting.

31

Proper*ties,* she thought. The man had said he owned *properties,* not just one, several. And he couldn't be more than forty.

Sal let herself into the chicken coop and promptly let herself back out again. She frowned. It was absurd to permit herself to get so excited about a man in a three-piece raw silk suit.

When she got to the kitchen, she stood for a moment clutching her aching side. Her hair had escaped from its knot and her face was deeply flushed and damp from running. She had pictured her absentee landlord as a group of paunchy, balding businessmen sitting around a long mahogany table in a stuffy oak-paneled boardroom with moose heads on the walls. She heard the car door slam, reached for two clean mugs and set them on the beat-up red Formica table. Robert Capolla had seemed familiar to her. Now, putting a name to the dramatically handsome face, that sense of familiarity was even stronger.

Sal was positive his name had not appeared on her lease. The name on the lease had been . . . Hopewell Corporation. Yes, that was it. Hopewell Corporation was stamped, and next to it Harry O'Brien had written his name. Harry O'Brien for Hopewell Corporation.

She shivered, but it was a delicious hot shiver that had nothing whatsoever to do with the weather. The memory of Robert Capolla's eyes on her was like an aphrodisiac. She felt short of breath, giddy. Maybe, she thought, she was hungry.

She grabbed a box of saltines, put them on a plate and grinned: some spread for a man in a raw silk suit. She'd been putting off going to the store for a week and was down to her last can of tuna fish, and only a tablespoon of peanut butter.

She jumped when he tapped at the back door. "It's

open!" She did not turn around, but heard his footsteps on the old pine floor and felt his presence.

"It doesn't bother you staying way out here all by yourself?" he asked as he sat down at the table, removed his jacket, and hung it on the back of the chair.

"In the beginning I was terrified." Sal poured coffee and sat down across from him. "Here I thought I was such a big girl, independent, liberated, and all that. The first few weeks I don't think I got more than a few hours sleep a night. And then I wouldn't doze off till it was light—as if the light could protect me. I even thought about ghosts," she drawled on in her honey-coated southern voice. "Good Lord, I hadn't thought about ghosts since I was a kid. But alone in . . . in *your* house I sure thought of them. I considered goin' down to the county courthouse and diggin' out some old records to see if some heinous crime had been committed within these walls. And I always thought of myself as a pragmatist!"

Robert laughed. "Sometimes we don't know who we are till we find ourselves in a difficult situation."

Sal sipped her coffee thoughtfully. She spread her hands out on the table, then caught sight of her ragged fingernails—at the dirt mixed with green paint—and removed them quickly.

"Since I came here," she went on, "I've had to overcome a lot of fears. I came for solitude yet discovered quickly that there's an art to living alone—it takes practice like everything else."

Robert's dark eyes inflamed her with another inquiring look. "Why do you need to be alone? Why is that so important?"

"So I can paint. So I can have the time to see, to really know what it is I want to paint. And to learn how

33

to translate my unique vision—" She broke off, embarrassed.

"Please . . . go on." He touched her arm with one finger, urging her to continue.

It was so easy to talk to him, yet she felt herself closing up. She sat for a moment, silently staring into her coffee cup. "That's really all there is to it," she said a minute later, then went to the stove for the coffee pot.

"You're very protective of that part of your life," Robert observed.

"Maybe." Sal leaned over and refilled his cup. The faint aroma of some deep, exotic, spicy scent tantalized her. Robert Capolla from New York City. Where had she heard that name before? she wondered. Had she read it somewhere?

Sal sat back down. "Let's say I'm just getting reacquainted with who I am. I've been away from serious art work since college. Mostly what I need is time. Not to be rushed, to simply allow the days to run their course, and to always, *always* work."

"You paint every day?" Robert inquired.

"Of course!"

"Well, I didn't know. I thought with all the work you must have to do—"

"That's the thing!" Sal interjected. "I have to paint every day. That's the only way things really start to happen. And I have to have tons of space to sprawl everything all over without feeling obliged to live an orderly sort of life . . . which is, by the way, why I'm offering you saltines and coffee. If you'd come a day later I'd have been out of coffee too."

"So you just paint and farm and have no obligations." Robert leaned back in his chair and scrutinized her with a hard, unyielding look.

She could see that he could be tough. Obviously he'd

34

had to be tough, she thought, to achieve his present status in whatever business he was in. Or maybe he had inherited his money. But she didn't think so. There was a ruggedness about him that people born into a lot of money did not usually have. No, she pegged him as a fighter, as someone who survived and won by wit and remarkable intellect.

"Oh, I have plenty of obligations," Sal said after a moment. "To myself."

"Of course." Robert's jaw tightened and the earlier shaded look came into his eyes. For a moment he seemed to be thinking of something else, his face drawn into a deeply concentrated expression that was very nearly a scowl. The room was oppressive.

He looked up suddenly. "They're the trickiest, don't you think? I mean obligations to oneself. They are really . . . the trickiest."

Sal nodded. Something was weighing on him heavily. She shifted in her chair, wondering again if he had been entirely truthful about his reasons for showing up so unexpectedly. With this sort of man one could never be sure.

"I admire you." He reached for a saltine and munched it as his expression softened. "You gave up something to move out here and become an artist. You took a risk. I could tell you were a risk-taker."

"I had my own advertising agency in Chicago," Sal offered. "What about you?"

"Why talk about me when we can talk about you? I'm serious. I think it's incredible what you're doing. You're a real pioneer woman."

Sal felt uneasy with his compliments.

"And nobody helps you?" He looked around as if a troop of dwarfs might pop out from behind the laboring refrigerator.

"Two teenagers." Sal laughed. "Sometimes *help* is not the best word for what they do. Sometimes they provide more comic relief than actual assistance."

He shifted his lean body, turning sideways in the chair, stretching his legs out in front of him. "Would you mind if I removed my tie?"

"Look at me." Sal gestured broadly with both arms. "Do I look like I would mind? We are not exactly having champagne and caviar in some chic little hideaway. I am not exactly wearin' my Sunday best!"

Sal averted her eyes as he loosened his tie and unbuttoned the top button of his white shirt. How on earth did he manage to look so crisp and cool on such a sweltering day? she wondered.

There was a magnetism about him that kept setting off jagged hot sensations along her inner arms. She pressed her legs together beneath the table as he got up and moved over to look out the window above the kitchen sink. Her whole body felt weakened, warm, and woozy. She reached for a saltine.

"Going to storm," he said, still staring out the window.

"Yes." She tried to dismiss the erotic twirling in the pit of her stomach. He was, after all, the sort of man she had long ceased to admire. Except for those rare moments when his face softened into a relaxed smile, he brought back far too many memories of the businessmen she had encountered in Chicago. And she had definitely had enough of men for whom money and power was everything.

Her mouth tightened as she recalled the backbiting, the underhanded competitiveness which several of her associates had used against her when she was in her ascendency. As soon as it had become apparent that she was more than a tall blonde with a pretty face, that she was in fact a creative force to be reckoned with, the very men who had flirted with her had united and turned against her. Well, not all of them, she amended, but most of them; enough of them to have soured her on the possibilities of finding anything remotely resembling a sensitive soul beneath the slick, corporate facade.

Yes, she thought, and that included anyone who wore a three-piece raw silk suit in ninety degree weather, in the country at that. She imagined his life in New York —a Park Avenue penthouse, limo, all of the sophisticated accoutrements of success. His wife, if he had one, would wear Gucci shoes; his children, if he had them, would definitely go to snobbish private schools, about which he would know nothing because that would surely be his wife's responsibility. But he didn't seem married to Sal, because she sensed he'd been sending out thinly veiled seductive signals ever since he arrived. She knew that type too. The type who *had to* flirt, the type who had to keep reminding a woman that he was a man, and she was a woman—as if that was always the most important distinction.

Sal noticed he wore a small emerald-cut diamond ring on his little finger, and she had to admit that was a bit quirky. Most three-piece-suiters did not risk a hint of glitz. But then, Robert Capolla was on a higher level than most of the men she had known in Chicago who were still scrambling up the slippery ladder to success. Robert Capolla was already there. Robert Capolla was big-money rich.

"What's the matter?" He returned to the table and gave her a careful look.

"Nothing." She tried to smile. No, she thought, it wasn't possible that he had sensed her negative thoughts about him.

37

"I was just thinking. . . ." she offered as he sat down. She felt his eyes scanning her face.

"You're very young to own all this," she said, looking up at him. There was nothing coy or naive in her observation. It was simply a fact, and Robert nodded. He seemed to approve of her direct approach. He sat back, waiting for the next move with the patient smile of an experienced gamesman.

"Where have I seen you before?" Sal leaned forward emphatically. The way he looked now, with that slightly arrogant half-smile . . . she was sure she'd seen that look before, maybe in a newspaper . . . or a magazine.

"Have we met? We haven't. . . ." She shook her head. "Have we? I usually have a good memory for faces but . . ."

"She asks the questions," Robert chuckled, "and she answers them. No wonder you want to be alone. You're perfectly capable of carrying on a conversation by yourself."

Sal laughed. "I've been told I lack a certain subtlety. That discreet finesse identified with us southerners is something that has always escaped me."

"I get enough finesse in my business," Robert observed with a hint of cynicism.

"Good Lord." Sal slammed her hand down on the table. "I know who you are. You're the man with the new car."

Robert's face crinkled into that delightful smile which so disarmed and warmed her. "I've never heard it put quite like that. You know, I think I see why you were a hit in advertising."

"Because I'm so simple." Sal smiled broadly. "Touché."

Of course she knew who he was, and now she remembered where she'd seen his picture. He had been on the cover of *Time* magazine as one of a small number of business moguls who had made a million dollars or more before they were forty years old. Yes, it was all coming back to her. Robert Capolla was, as she had instinctively felt, a self-made man. The son of poor Italian immigrants, he had graduated from Harvard at nineteen and made millions of dollars by the time he was thirty-five. At present he was involved in perfecting a new battery-operated automobile which some auto industry analysts believed would revolutionize the whole industry.

"The world awaits the Capolla car. Right? This must be a very exciting time for you. How do you find time to check in on your rural outposts?"

"Am I insulted?" Robert gave her a defensive look.

"Oh, no!" Sal reached instinctively for his hand to take the sting out of her candid observation. She had not meant to insult him.

The touch of his warm, smooth skin sent a tremor up her spine and she released his hand instantly, as if she had been burned. For a moment they were both silent. She knew he had been as keenly aware of the electric pulses passing between them as she was.

"Yes, it is an exciting time." He reassumed their conversation and began to explain his project. When he talked about the car his face took on a rapturous, excited expression which made him seem more a young man of twenty than a man in his early forties who occasionally looked older. There was something thrilling about the way he spoke of the car and what it might mean in terms of a far-reaching benefit to the environment.

As he continued, she tried to recall other details from the *Time* article. Marriage? Yes, he had been married several times. Well, maybe only twice—she couldn't remember exactly. And he had children, several children, one of whom was a teenager, which indicated he'd been married young. The article had also alluded to his fondness for women, painting a bold picture of him as a dashing international lover. If she was not mistaken, his current marital status was divorced.

"Now tell me more about your painting." He had stopped talking about his car abruptly, as if some disquieting thought had crossed his mind. "What gallery handles your work?"

"I'm afraid that's jumpin' the gun," Sal told him.

"You need a gallery." His face took on a preoccupied look.

Sal gaped at him. Good Lord, he was already trying to manage her life.

"I'll take your slides, if you have any, back to my attorney. He represents several up-and-coming artists. You may know that's the way it's quite often done—through attorneys, acting as agents. I'd be glad to help you."

"But you haven't even seen—"

"I can tell you're good," Robert confirmed powerfully.

Sal pressed her lips together. So now she had seen the dynamic man in action, a veritable whirlwind. Well, she had no doubt he could place her paintings in some New York gallery, whether they were any good or not.

"Thank you." She got up slowly from the table and crossed over to the stove. "That's very kind of you." She drew in a deep breath, astonished at how disappointed she felt at his lack of sensitivity. "I'm afraid I'm not ready to show my work yet." She gave him a staunch look. Too bad she had to see him this way. The men she'd dated in Chicago had mostly bored her. It had been years since she'd felt such excitement with a man.

"You're too modest." Robert was firm—the voice of authority.

"I'm not modest," Sal reproached him slightly.

"You're modest about your beauty." He leaned back in his chair, daring it to topple over.

Sal ignored him, and moved to the sink to rinse out the coffee pot. So his offer to take her slides to New York had been nothing more than an easy come-on, just more smalltalk—typical jargon to let her know how much influence he wielded.

"Mr. Capolla," she said evenly with her back to him, "what do you really want? Why did you really come over here today?"

She turned around to find him grinning up at her from his precariously tilted chair. "I came to see if I could get you out of here without a fight." His dark eyes sparkled.

Sal did not blink. She nodded and turned back to the sink before opening her mouth to exhale an irate breath. Damn, if she hadn't been right about him all along! A man as important and busy as Robert Capolla did not waste an afternoon chatting over saltines and coffee.

"Only I've changed my mind." He moved to stand next to her at the sink.

She shot him a dubious look, and he laughed.

"You're not sure you like me, are you?" he asked her.

Sal put the coffee pot into the dish drain. The question was too personal. She wanted this conversation steered immediately back onto something trivial. She didn't trust him, but *like* was another matter. The damn thing was she *did* like him.

"I bet you were a helluva businesswoman!" His voice rang out boisterously, and somewhere deep inside she quivered to the hearty masculine sound. Well, one thing the afternoon had brought home was that she had been alone too long. She definitely needed male companionship. Only she didn't need Robert Capolla, she thought, or anyone like him.

"Actually, I came over here to see if I could get you to move over into one of my other houses. I was thinking about selling this place."

"That's up to you." Sal's body flushed hot as his bare arm brushed against her elbow. "I'm not going to waste my time in some futile legal entanglement . . . in fighting you, as you put it."

"But I said I wasn't going to—"

"Thank you." She whirled around and faced him.

"You're not as easygoing as you seem." He took a step forward and looked into her eyes. "Or as you would like people to believe."

"I don't like to be toyed with. . . ."

"I honestly wasn't." Robert's breath was warm on her face. "Just like you didn't mean to insult me earlier."

Sal felt a knot of emotion rise in her throat. There was a gentleness about him now that made her yearn to know more about him. Outside, the thunder was rolling in closer and closer and the smoky sky had deepened so that it was almost dark. They both turned to look out the window, watching the trees dip and strain in the wind.

Sal's heart was pounding as violently as the thunder that roared and shook the old house. A jagged streak of lightning cut through the sky, the dark world of swirling leaves and silver rain tinged with a greenish brilliance. Sal hugged her arms in front of her breasts. Their shoulders were barely touching, yet she was keenly aware of every breath he drew. The power of the storm seemed to be raging in them both.

They both jumped at a deafening crack of thunder. "One, two, three . . ." Sal counted under her breath, timing the claps to see how close the eye of the storm was to the house. Another blinding flash, and with it a deluge slashed against the window. She glanced quickly at Robert. He was mesmerized by the storm, his body taut.

"Beautiful." His sigh triggered a deep yearning. It was as if he had caressed her. But, of course, he was speaking of the storm. Sal moved slowly back to the red Formica table and sat down, nibbling on a saltine.

She watched his motionless back, the broad shoulders, lean torso, slender hips. After another deafening rumble he returned to his chair, picked up another saltine and munched it. The pupils of his dark eyes were dilated and he bore the intense look of someone in a trance. He seemed totally oblivious to her. Perhaps, she thought, he was thinking about some technical problem concerning his automotive invention.

"Sorry." He shook himself back to present realities and gave her a charming smile.

"That's all right." Sal met his eyes, wondering what he had been thinking.

His charming smile softened to something gentler, and he reached for another saltine. "I haven't had one of these since I was a kid. They're damn good."

"I keep them in the broiler of the stove. The pilot light keeps them from going stale in all this humidity." Sal could not draw her eyes away from his. For a moment the storm outside ceased to exist and they were locked in the thrall of a deep silence of their own creation.

43

"Am I a villain or a respectable businessman in your mind, Sal Carter?"

Sal smiled softly. She liked him best when he was blunt.

"People like me, who make quick money, are either loved or hated, condemned for being scoundrels or idolized as saviors of a crumbling capitalistic system."

"I don't think anyone's a scoundrel just because they have a talent for making money," Sal said. "I guess it depends on how they made it and what they do with the money once they have it. Believe it or not, I had a talent for making money too. Oh, I'm not in your league, but my agency in Chicago did, and is doing pretty well."

"So you won't reject me because of my money." Robert smiled warmly. "That's a relief." He winked at her, but for all the lightness he felt, he was relieved.

"Are you married?" Sal thrust her chin forward as she asked the question. Her hands were damp with perspiration, and she unconsciously crossed the fingers on both hands. This was ridiculous, she thought. He lived in New York City. She woud never see him again. As soon as the rain slowed down he would be gone.

"Not at the moment. Anything in mind?"

Sal shook her head and laughed. Now it was her turn to be relieved. "But you have been. How many times?"

"You're going to find something to hold against me." Robert sighed. "I just know you are. You're a high-minded moral person . . . just the type of woman I swore I'd never get involved with."

Sal chuckled. They both seemed to relish trading insults with each other. "You're not involved."

"Oh?" Robert raised a thick eyebrow. "Yes I am . . . with you."

Sal felt a rush of maddening sensations inflame her. She stood up, crossed over to the stove and emptied the rest of the saltines onto the plate. When she returned to the table he reached for her hand. The sensation mesmerized her, and for several minutes she sat stiffly with her hand encased in his, listening to the steady downpour outside.

"Fly to New York next weekend." He gave her hand an imperative squeeze and then released it.

"Just like that?" Sal tried to laugh him off, but her pulse was racing wildly at the idea.

"I'll send my plane." He reached for her hand again, but she avoided his clasp.

"Do you always proposition women you've known only a few minutes?" she accused him good-naturedly.

"Not always." He wrinkled his brow. "Come to New York. How long has it been since you've been to the Big Apple? And I'm the guy to show you the city. We'll go to museums . . . do arty things. I promise you . . ."

". . . a good time!" Sal tossed back her head. She felt like leaping out of her chair to dispel the agonizing sensations his invitation evoked.

"You deserve time off from all this," he went on persuasively. "Leave your cows behind." He was an appealing and convincing clown. "Put a gone fishin' sign on your vegetable stand and let your easel rest. You won't have to think about a thing. No hassle. That's what money's for. My plane, my car . . . me . . . all at your disposal!"

Before Sal could reply, a blast of Beethoven's Pastoral Symphony shook the house with the same force as the earlier storm.

"Just a minute." Sal excused herself and dashed up the narrow back kitchen stairs. She had completely forgotten about Abe.

She peeked in one studio, and not finding him there, looked in the other room he used. She called out to him,

45

but apparently he had gone down the front staircase. By the time she reached the kitchen, Robert was standing next to the door with a tight smile on his face.

"This is my friend Abe." Sal rushed forward to explain.

"Yes, we've just met." Robert slung his jacket over his shoulder and opened the door to the steaming, dripping world outside.

"Sorry about the blast of Beethoven," Abe apologized as he disappeared up the rear stairs.

"He uses two of the upstairs rooms as studios to paint in." Sal was stunned by the sudden stony attitude that had overtaken him. She opened her mouth to explain further, then stopped herself. She owed Robert Capolla no explanations. Did he think she and Abe were living together? Had he learned so little about her during their afternoon together that that was his narrow-minded conclusion?

"Listen"—he gave her a curt look—"I'll call you later."

"Don't you want an umbrella?" Sal leaned out the door. He was already dashing toward the car.

"I'm staying at the Boar's Head." He ducked into the vehicle.

"Damn!" Sal let out a livid sigh as he turned over the engine. Her head was reeling. She went back inside and glanced up at the kitchen clock. She could hardly believe that they'd been talking for an hour and a half. The time had flown by, and he'd certainly flown out of there very suddenly.

She collapsed into a chair and immediately jumped to her feet. Did he really think she had been toying with him while her husband or lover was upstairs? Or maybe, she thought, he was so accustomed to women falling all over him that her hesitation over his proposed weekend in New York had put him off. She frowned. Damn him for unsettling her so!

Sal crossed back to the kitchen door, but he had already driven off. Suddenly, Sal's mouth flew open and she felt a panic she had not felt in months. He couldn't call her! She didn't have a damn phone!

CHAPTER THREE

"I must be an idiot!" Three hours later she was pacing around Abe's studio, chastising herself. "He said he'd call and I just gaped at him like a lunatic. I must have behaved like . . . Oh, I can't stand thinking about it. Abe! Listen to me."

"How can I not listen to you?" Abe stuck one brush in his mouth and picked up another to add a few touches of zinc white to his canvas. "You've been berating yourself for hours."

"Well, he owns the place." Sal flopped down on the floor in one corner of the room.

"Then he knows where to find you," Abe said.

"He'll try to call . . . find out I'm not listed . . . think I didn't want him to call, and that will be that. He already thinks you're my lover or—"

"So go over to the Boar's Head Inn. It's not that late. I've never seen you so upset."

"I'm not upset," Sal denied, and folded her arms stubbornly in front of her aching breasts.

48

She bolted off the floor and walked over to a window with her hands jammed into the pockets of a clean pair of jeans.

"Sal, just drive on over to the Inn. If you don't want to ring his room, leave a message at the desk."

Sal stared out into the dark night. The rain had finally stopped and things were a bit cooler than before. But by tomorrow it would be steaming again.

"I'll even shower and put on a clean shirt and come with you." Abe moved to her side and put a friendly arm around her. "What did that guy do to elicit—"

"He didn't do anything," Sal snapped, then noting Abe's skepticism, she laughed. "Oh, all right. I am *slightly* attracted to him."

"I'd say you were daffy. I don't understand, Sal. That man—"

"Robert Capolla."

"Yes, Robert Capolla. That man is cut precisely from the corporate mold. I thought you were trying to get away from that sort of thing."

"He's not *at all* cut from any mold," Sal protested. "Okay. I know how it looks. I thought so too when I first saw him but—"

"Listen to me." Abe put a restraining arm on her shoulder. "You've been working too hard. You won't even cut loose on Saturday nights. You've been living like a hermit out here. You've hardly had a decent conversation with anyone in six months."

"A love-starved, sex-starved fool." Sal batted her lashes at Abe, refusing to take him seriously.

"He just doesn't seem like your type," Abe called as she walked out of the room.

Maybe Abe was right, she thought. Maybe she was overreacting. Maybe it was just as well if Robert thought she was involved with Abe and wasn't interested in seeing him.

She moved slowly through the dark kitchen. There was one saltine left and she fingered it gently, as if it contained some magical remedy for the loneliness she felt.

The next morning she woke earlier than usual and performed most of her chores in the gray, murky, predawn silence. Her body felt tense and stiff. She could tell by the stillness in the air that the day was going to be stifling and sultry, and that probably there would be intermittent showers.

She decided Abe was right: She had been working too hard. Well, she would take the day off. With the low pressure system hovering over the area, it would not be a good day for painting outside anyway.

Sal sat at the kitchen table, sipping coffee and making a feeble attempt at composing a grocery list. She really should go into Charlottesville to shop and to go to the bank, she told herself. She should also stop by O'Brien Realty to check out any new listings. And maybe, just *maybe* she would drop by the Boar's Head Inn and leave a message for Robert, in case he came out while she was away.

But Sal could not get herself to move, and when Abe drove in around noon she ran to the window, thinking it might be Robert.

"Severe thunderstorms are forecast all over the valley," Abe announced. "If you want to get any work done you'd better start painting before it's too dark to see and we lose power. Also, Dorie wants you to come for dinner tonight. She's invited the physics professor."

"You must think I'm in rotten shape." Sal trailed Abe up to his studio and watched him squeeze fresh paint onto his palette.

"I just hate to see you mooning over some shiny-shoed stranger. Next thing I know you'll be having a phone installed."

Sal laughed. "Wrong!"

She marched out of Abe's room and into her own studio. She would forget about Robert Capolla and damn the groceries and the bank. She was not going to have her life disrupted by, as Abe had phrased it, a shiny-shoed stranger.

"Okay," she yelled out to Abe, "I accept dinner. What time?"

"Eight thirty!" Abe yelled back.

Fine, good, she told herself—forget about Robert Capolla. She spent the next four hours painting, and when thunder struck and the lights went out, she fell into her bed and napped for the rest of the afternoon.

She woke at six, chilled and anxious, with one thought predominant in her mind. Robert Capolla had not stopped by. Well, she was better off! she decided.

Sal dressed for the evening in a full, softly pleated brown cotton skirt which she wore with a brown and orange backless blouse and flat leather sandals. Then she drove into town to meet the physics professor. As she drove past the Boar's Head Inn she was tempted to stop in, just to see if Robert Capolla had already checked out.

Don't! she told herself. Obviously, he had just been indulging in some impromptu fireworks yesterday. She thought she would look like a fool if she stopped by, especially now—dressed up and smelling of her best French perfume.

Actually, the evening with Dorie, Abe's girlfriend, and Abe and the physics professor, proved far more enjoyable and relaxing than she had anticipated. Leo Forrestor was a fascinating man—tall and blond, charming and loquacious. He was all the things that might have interested her and, she admitted to herself as she drove home around eleven that night, he might interest her in the future, once the memory of Robert Capolla faded. In fact, she had accepted a date with him for the following Saturday night.

As she passed the Boar's Head for the second time that night, the impulse to stop overpowered her. Perhaps it was the wine that made her feel bold, she thought. In any case, she found herself striding into the lobby, smiling at the night clerk and inquiring about Mr. Capolla.

"I'm almost certain I saw him go out earlier," the clerk replied. "Shall I ring his room, just in case?"

What was she going to say if he was there? she wondered. Would she go to his room? Would she meet him in the bar? Or maybe she'd just make up some story. She sighed. If only she were the type who could invent, fabricate, or even distort the truth slightly.

"Please," Sal responded. Her heart seemed about to burst as the clerk dialed the phone.

"Ah, yes, Mrs. Capolla. Is your husband there?"

Sal's eyes flew open and her jaw dropped. *Mrs. Capolla?* She clutched the desk to keep from bolting.

"I see. . . ." The clerk smiled and nodded in response to the reply. "There's a . . . someone to see him. Shall I just take a message, then, or shall I send her up to wait?"

To wait? For an instant Sal thought her legs were going to buckle under her. She shook her head, signaling the clerk that she was in a hurry, that she would leave a message. When he hung up, she scribbled some gibberish on a piece of paper, slipped it in an envelope, and handed it to him with a smile she knew was far too broad. She really was rotten at pretense.

Damn! All the way home she fumed at herself for being so stupid. Imagine him coming out to her house, flirting with her, and then actually proposing she spend the weekend in New York with him while his wife was waiting for him back at the hotel! Abe was right, she thought. He was cut from the same mold—only worse. Unfeeling, conniving, hellbent on getting his own way—a complete egomaniac.

Sal gunned her old Ford station wagon up the driveway, slamming on her brakes, when she caught sight of the black Porsche. What the hell was he doing here?

She rolled down the window and craned her neck. He was sitting on the back step, smoking a cigarette. Waiting. She resisted the urge to yell something at him and hopped out of her car with her fists clenched.

Who the hell did he think he was? she fumed. What had he told his wife? Her breath was coming in hot, angry gasps. She had never been so furious in her life. She was not by nature an angry person. She could hardly remember the last time she had lost her temper.

"Look, I'll try to be civil," Sal snapped out loud as she approached the seated figure.

"You don't have a phone." He stood up and eyed her suspiciously. "Was that some kind of joke?"

"What . . . ?" Sal knew she was feeling too angry and disappointed to behave civilly.

"I said"—Robert's dark eyes were troubled—"were you joking when you told me to call you?"

"I didn't tell you to call me," Sal jumped in. *"You* said you would call me."

"You didn't correct me, did you?"

"No, I didn't," Sal said tightly. Let him think what he wanted to think. Let him think she had a lover and that she was trying to make a fool of him. He had lived so long in a world where all people could do was play games that he was probably incapable of simple, honest communication. She didn't have time for such convoluted dealings.

"Sal . . ." He reached out for her but she stiffened and he moved back.

"You don't have any right coming out here like this so late at night. You own the place but I pay you money to rent it."

"I came out several times," he said rigidly. "How the hell are you supposed to communicate with someone who doesn't have a phone?"

"By letter." Sal met his eyes directly for the first time that evening.

Why didn't you tell me you were married! She wanted to hurl the words at him. Instead she climbed the porch steps and leaned against the railing, looking up at the stars. "I stopped by the Boar's Head Inn." She dropped the information in a soft, unemotional voice. The silence which followed made her stomach churn, only now she was no longer angry. Suddenly she felt saddened by his deception. "I heard about your wife."

"I'd like to explain." He mounted the porch steps slowly.

"You don't owe me any explanation," Sal said wearily. She wanted nothing more personal to take place between them, wanted only for him to disappear from her life.

"Do you think I would have invited you to New York if I was married?" he asked in a sullen voice that mirrored her own encroaching depression.

"You thought I was plying you with saltines and coffee, with my lover or my husband upstairs." She shook her head at the preposterousness of it all. Simplicity was what she wanted.

"It did seem a bit odd," he replied. "A rather good-

54

looking man popping down from upstairs? It wasn't entirely an outlandish assumption, was it?"

Sal closed her eyes. It was too complicated. She wanted none of it. "Why did you come back out then? If it's business, we can take care of things through Gabby. If you've changed your mind about letting me stay on here, that's fine, I'll find something else."

"I didn't think you'd give up so easily."

Sal turned to him with an unruffled expression. "I don't give up easily. I also don't get involved in battles just for the sake of winning. I don't have that much at stake."

"Is that why you think I came back out here?" He faced her squarely, and once again she was painfully aware of his overwhelming masculinity.

"You think I came back out because I've made you into some sort of conquest? What if I said I came back out here because I enjoyed myself more yesterday afternoon than I have in—"

"You have a wife," Sal interrupted. "She was no doubt waiting for you while you were—"

"Damn it! I'm not married to her anymore. We've been divorced for four years."

"Don't explain!" Sal hopped off the railing. It was all happening again—the racing pulse, the desire.

He stepped in front of her. "I don't have a wife. I don't have a fiancée. I am not here to ask you to move out. I want to see you again."

Sal felt herself waiver. What if he was telling the truth?

"Sal, I have to go back to New York the first thing tomorrow morning. I want to see you again. I know it's no good asking you to fly to New York after all this confusion, but I'd like to see you next Saturday. I'll fly back down here."

Sal drew in a deep breath. Isn't that just what she'd wanted to hear? she asked herself. But a wife, or rather an ex-wife—it was all too complicated.

"You never asked for a further explanation about Abe," she noted wryly.

"I phoned Harry O'Brien at his home, asked if you were married, asked if you were the sole tenant of my property. He told me about Abe."

"I suppose you were within your rights to inquire." Sal felt drained. No, she told herself, she didn't care. She knew it was wise to let this man go.

"Don't come back down on my account." She gave him a guarded look as she crossed to the back door.

"No hard feelings." She extended her hand to him, and when he took it in his, she ignored the warm pressure of his response. "Good luck with your new car." She went inside and heard him drive away.

"What's got into you?" Abe asked several days later when he came in for the third day in a row and found her cooking eggs and bacon for breakfast.

"New leaf." Sal stood at the stove wearing her faded blue overalls. Having completed her morning chores, she had showered and braided her hair into two fat pigtails.

"You were right as usual, Abe. I was becoming a recluse. Also a bit of a slob. Eating irregularly, living a basically slipshod existence. Voilà! . . ."

Sal moved to the old refrigerator and threw it open, revealing its stunningly well-stocked contents. "I'm inviting you, Dorie, and Leo to dinner on Sunday. I'll also ask Martha and Skip," she added, referring to her closest neighbors.

"Well, I'll be damned." Abe gave her a friendly peck on the cheek.

She smiled. Yes, she was turning over a new leaf. Her encounter with Robert Capolla had proved to her how vulnerable she was, how one-sided and distorted her life had become. If she had been so carried away by such an obvious phony, she reasoned, she must have really been in bad shape. Abe had hit the nail on the head. In a way she had been a love-starved fool. She was determined to change things!

Later the following afternoon, after a productive day of painting down by the stream, Sal showered and slipped into a pair of white trousers and a white T-shirt. Abe had left for the day. She poured herself a glass of white wine and sat in the old rocker on the side porch, admiring the sunset.

There were two enormous willow trees down where the side lawn sloped toward a slow trickling stream, and she watched their pale fronds fluttering in the violet hues of evening. Her body ached but she felt it was a good aching, clean and sharp. Not like the tight fatigue she had experienced at the end of her workdays in Chicago. In spite of it all, she felt good. Actually, she thought, she had Robert Capolla to thank for bringing her to her senses. She had been turning into a workhorse. Her obsession with farming and her art had, in a way, been no different from her workaholic compulsions in Chicago.

Sal went back inside to refill her wineglass. When she returned to the rocker the crunch of gravel signaled the arrival of some unexpected visitor.

The black Porsche—she couldn't believe it.

She drew in a deep breath, sipped her wine, and watched him mount the steps to the side porch. The immaculate white jacket he wore made him appear even darker, like an Arabian prince. What could he possibly be up to now? she wondered.

"I thought you went back to New York."

"I did." Robert sat on the porch railing, facing her. "Something has come up this Saturday so I won't be able to come down then. I have to leave the country on business. I wanted to clear things up with you."

"But they're cleared up." Sal forced her fingers to loosen their grip on the stem of the wineglass. "They really are."

"Do you mind if I go inside and pour myself a glass of wine?" He gave her a tentative smile and she had to resist responding in kind: He could be so damn appealing!

"I'll get you some wine." Sal rose, went inside, and returned with a glass.

"Thank you," he said when she returned, accepting the wine with a guarded smile.

"You're making too much of this." Sal sat down and began rocking slowly to soothe the persistent tugging in her stomach and the fluttering pulse—the sensations Robert Capolla evoked in her. So what if she was attracted to him? she thought. She had long since grown out of the adolescent belief that a throbbing heart signaled true love.

"I disagree with you," Robert said. "How often do you meet someone who really captures your imagination, who fires you in some inexplicable way?"

Not often. Sal raised her eyes briefly in the slightest indication that he might have a point.

"You captured my imagination." He took up his position on the porch railing, adjusting his perfectly creased navy-blue trousers as he did. His shoes were white and as immaculate as his jacket. Usually she didn't like men in white shoes, but his were a soft comfortable-looking leather and she found herself admiring their simple elegant lines.

"A brilliant, beautiful young woman like you, who gives up a successful business—yes, I checked on that too—and decides to combine farming and art . . . ? I'd say that bears looking into."

"And you're looking into it?" Sal gave him a dubious look.

"Yes." He lavished one of his most charming smiles on her. "I knew you were far too angry the other night to listen, so I didn't press the issue."

"Well, thank you very much." Sal was trying not to feel flattered by his persistence. After all, she thought, he was clearly accomplished at using his sophisticated blarney to get what he wanted.

"And you think I've cooled off enough now to—"

"I hope so," Robert interrupted. The passionate gruffness in his voice made her look up. His face was drawn and worried. The practiced, charming expression was gone, his face was drawn and worried, as if a great deal were at stake.

"Well, you're right." Sal met his eyes honestly, stirred by his lack of pretense.

"When I came out here the other afternoon I had no idea I'd find someone like you. I'd come down with several things in mind. As I said, I'd decided to put this place on the market and I wanted to check into my other properties. And I came down, as I started to explain the other night, with my ex-wife. It was one of many attempts at a reconciliation."

Sal tensed as he continued. "When I met you I knew right there and then that I wanted you, and for us to get to know each other. The fact that my ex-wife was waiting for me at the Boar's Head had nothing to do with you. Don't you see? Maybe I stayed and talked with you too long, but the storm justified my hanging around even longer."

Sal shivered. Did she really want to hear all of this? Wasn't she just opening herself up for a lot of unhappiness? Did she really need a situation fraught with such complications—ex-wives, reconciliations, and who knew what other emotional entanglements?

"When that man . . . when Abe came downstairs it totally threw me. I admit I reacted badly. Jealousy overwhelmed me."

"Please stop!" Sal interrupted in a low whisper.

"No, no," Robert topped her, "you're getting the wrong impression. This attempt at reconciliation was something Marilyn and I had tried before, for the sake of the children. I think we both knew before we came down that it was futile. It was my idea, actually. A reconciliation, I thought, would be good for the children. We have two. They live in London with Marilyn. I miss them. I guess I deluded myself—" He broke off and was silent for several minutes.

Sal resisted a strong impulse to reach out to him. She was trying desperately to remain aloof, to listen to his story with the cool objectivity of a stranger.

She took a long sip of wine. Why did she feel that she knew him? she wondered. Why had he, from the moment she'd seen him, seemed so remarkably familiar to her? She had told herself it was because he reminded her of all those ambitious, power-obsessed men she had known in Chicago. And that was partly true. But she had also recognized something else in him—something razor-sharp, pure, and fine. She had recognized a part of herself in him. Although they had talked only a short time, she detected a kindred soul beneath the slick exterior. She, too, knew what it was to feel driven to accomplish something of value. No, she thought, she had never felt it about the business in Chicago. But she felt it here, about her art, and the farm too.

"Marilyn and I have been divorced for four years," Robert said, breaking the long silence. "I won't whitewash myself and pretend that the dissolution of our marriage was all her fault. I'd say it was mutual, though I can see you don't believe me. You do think I'm a scoundrel, not to be trusted."

Sal shook her head. "I don't know what I think."

"I am telling you the truth now. I flew all the way back to do it. That's got to count for something."

Maybe, maybe not, Sal reflected. She did believe him, and believed that for some reason he wanted her to think well of him. But his impetuous style made her balk. Maybe he was just another man who liked a challenge, she thought, a man who needed to prove to himself that there was nothing or no one he couldn't have. New York City was filled with beautiful, intelligent women. He didn't need to go flying off to the Shenandoah Valley to find an interesting companion. No, she could see he was a man who always made a ruckus. His flashy, exotic appearance was an indication of how he saw himself, of the impression he wished to give. Sal smiled wryly. And maybe he'd never met a woman farmer before. It was probably as simple as that.

Only it wasn't as simple as that. Looking at the purple range of mountains in the distance, Sal wondered if she was naive to think that it had been difficult for him to tell her what he'd just told her.

"Can't we just forget the mix-up?" he asked her finally.

She met his eyes for a moment and then looked away. In a way, that was what she wanted: to forget his jealous reaction to Abe, to forget his ex-wife and the allusions the magazine article had made to his womanizing.

"Look, if your friend hadn't appeared, I wouldn't have gotten angry and left so suddenly! We'd have made another date, you wouldn't have stopped by the Boar's Head, discovered I was there with another woman, and concluded I was a liar, etcetera, etcetera. It might have been simpler."

"I have a feeling," Sal looked at him with troubled eyes, "that nothing is ever simple with you."

Robert's mouth tensed and the furrow between his heavy brows deepened. She had struck a soft spot. Suddenly, he grinned. "You see! You *do* know me."

Sal's heart quickened. He had simultaneously admitted his weakness and scored something of a victory. Yes, she did know him. She felt it too.

She recognized his intense curiosity, his impatience, and his almost superhuman physical energy. She recognized these qualities because she herself possessed them. They were what had enabled her to rise to the top of the Chicago advertising world, and what now enabled her to pursue her art in solitude. Both she and Robert were driven—driven to accomplish certain things.

"I don't want my life to be as complicated as it has been," he went on seriously. "People change, don't they? They aspire to a more fulfilling life. That's what you did, wasn't it, when you left your business in Chicago?"

"Robert"—Sal inched away from him, resting her hands lightly on the porch railing—"you buy up property you've never seen, spend half your time in the air winging from one company to the other—"

"You do hold my life against me." Robert threw up his hands in frustration.

"I—I . . ." Sal paused with the truth sticking in her throat. "I'm afraid of you. I left your kind of life behind."

Robert drew in a long breath. His handsome face was drawn, and for the first time she noticed how very pale his skin was. Of course, he would be too busy to enjoy the sun. No, Robert Capolla was not a golf-playing or tennis-playing executive.

"I like you." Sal felt a twinge of sadness as she continued. "But . . . I can see that even a fling or a summer affair with you would be all-consuming. I don't need, or want, that sort of intensity in my life."

"You can really be that objective?" Robert caught her eye. Although they were not touching, she could feel the prickly heat all over her body.

"You like to dominate . . . everything." Sal's soft smile took the sting out of her words. "Business, of course, *and* your relationships. Be truthful. Didn't you really always expect your ex-wife to be there when you snapped your fingers?"

A smile flickered on Robert's mouth. "I have two ex-wives," he said. "And they both accused me of the same thing. Why is it that hearing it from you doesn't make me angry or defensive?"

"Because I'm not your wife." Sal laughed for the first time since he'd arrived.

"Marry me and you will be." Robert strained toward her.

Sal caught her breath. "Marry you?"

"I'm not joking." He tensed his large hands and the movement unleashed a series of wild erotic gyrations in her very core. He was dying to seize her, to hold her and consume her, yet he was holding himself back.

"Do you always propose the second time you—"

"No, I don't!" he interrupted gently. "My first wife was a childhood sweetheart . . . someone I'd known forever. I knew Marilyn ten years before—"

"Robert, please!" Sal raised her hand to silence him, but he grasped it and pressed it to his lips.

"I love you, Sal," he said, and his dark eyes mirrored the rich intensity of his feeling. "I love you and I want to marry you."

CHAPTER FOUR

"But you can't!" Sal shrank back into the rocking chair and tried to laugh. The vulnerability in his face, the high pitch of sensuality that existed between them made her tremble. And she had never, never before in her life trembled.

"You don't propose . . . you can't!" She shook her head as if she could dismiss everything lightly. "You can't love me!"

"Can." Robert pulled his chair around and straddled it backward, facing her. "And do." He smiled, folded his hands over the back of the chair, and sat calmly waiting for her reply.

"This can't be happening," Sal muttered half under her breath.

Robert laughed, a loud hearty laugh which reverberated in the hush of evening.

Sal stared at him incredulously. The intense, passionate vulnerability was gone and he was once again the confident, seductive charmer.

"I went back to New York, put in three eighteen-hour days at my office, and spent the evenings getting soused on Jack Daniel's with my earphones blasting that same damn Beethoven symphony that interrupted us the other afternoon. I told myself I had had no intention of coming back down here."

"That's what I thought." Sal considered him carefully.

"Only I couldn't stop thinking of you and your saltines and your damn strong coffee!"

A giggle bubbled out of Sal, and without thinking she reached out and clasped his hand.

"I went out to my local deli at four one morning to buy a box of saltines." Robert smiled.

"You're making this up!" Sal accused with a radiant smile.

"Not *all* of it!" Robert's dark eyes danced. "I *thought* about going out for the saltines but the Jack Daniel's had me too numbed. So tell me . . . did you think of me at all?"

"You know I did." Sal laced her fingers through his and her body surged hot at the delicious sensation of his soft skin.

"I want to get to know you," Robert said softly. "I have to be back in New York tomorrow morning. . . ."

"I can't rush!" Sal felt the panic rising in her throat. It seemed unreal to her—fraught with the sort of romantic fantasy she did not trust.

She groped for logical reasons why it was ridiculous to entertain thoughts of anything permanent happening between them. "I'm a farmer. And I'm an artist, Robert, not a wife who throws smashing dinner parties and says all the right things."

"I know." Robert hopped out of his chair and disappeared inside the house. He returned a moment later with the bottle of wine, sat down in the chair—the proper way this time—and stared out across the emerald green expanse, toward the mountains.

"This spot is magic. Old Tom Jefferson knew what he was doing."

"And you actually bought all this without seeing it?" Sal admired his strong profile.

"I'm forty-one years old," he said without looking at her. "I've bought a lot of things without seeing them. I've looked through a lot of people. You were right when you said nothing is simple for me. When I sat in your kitchen eating saltines and drinking coffee, it hit me that I hadn't felt so alive since I was a kid. I think nothing of blowing three or four hundred dollars on a dinner. Hell, more if I spring for a bottle of fancy wine. The wine alone can cost five hundred dollars. And yet your damn mud-thick coffee and your saltines fed some part of me that was starving."

Sal's skepticism surfaced again. It was difficult not to be flattered. After all, Robert Capolla was a phenomenon. Not that she thought he was lying. No, he truly believed everything he was saying—which was probably one of the reasons he was such a brilliant success in business, she thought. He possessed an uncanny talent for convincing, because, at any given moment, he desperately believed in whatever he was selling. She wondered if he had ever lost, if he had ever wanted something and seen it slip through his fingers.

"I have four children." He gave a self-deprecating smile. "I sometimes feel like a man who's been quartered—parts of me seem to have been dispersed over the earth. Two of my children live in London, two in Los Angeles. I live in New York but spend most of my time in Detroit or a small village outside of Venice. I own property in Virginia, Montana, Idaho, New York,

France, Italy, and St. Croix. Until I came back from here last week I thought I was getting an ulcer. The doctor has had me off coffee for six months, yet five cups of your mixture seemed like some miraculous cure."

"Robert, this is all very flattering." Sal stood up and walked slowly over to the porch railing. The violet shadows had deepened. The mountains were enveloped in an inky blue mist and several shimmering stars pierced through the layer of low clouds.

"You know I'm a poor risk," he said. "I just wanted to give you specifics, so you don't imagine me any worse than I am."

"You're wrong." She turned to him shyly. "I haven't turned you into a monster in my mind. Oh, I did let off some steam after I stopped by the Boar's Head, but I haven't heaped a lot of vituperation on you."

"I try to see my children as often as possible," he went on. "I wish they lived closer to me. I've tried to arrange it."

"You needn't keep explaining or justifying." Sal's voice was husky. She was deeply moved by his desire to convince her that he was more than a powerhouse, more than a mogul.

"I never intended to marry again." He receded into the shadows. "I do many things well. Marriage, I figured, was one of the things I do not do well."

"Let's please not talk about—"

"All right," he acquiesced, and for a moment they were caught in the thrall of the last deep purple shadows as the thick night noises began their rhythmic litany. Finally, they were enveloped in rich, velvety darkness.

"It's so beautiful here," Robert whispered in a voice that was now part of the nocturnal symphony.

68

Sal's breasts rose and fell beneath her white shirt and she was aware of every generous curve of her body and how it would feel to lie naked in his arms. She kept waiting for him to make a move but he continued to sit, his chair tilted at a slight angle, staring out at the black outline of the Shenandoah Mountains.

"What time do you get up in the morning?"

His question set off a collage of fiery images. "Around five," she said, thinking only of his lean, muscular arms embracing her, of the intensity of his sinewy body pressing into her.

"I have to fly back to New York," he offered after a moment. "As soon as it's light."

Sal swallowed the knot that had formed in her throat. Was she really prepared to share her bed with this man so soon? she asked herself. And if she did, wouldn't it be even more difficult to say good-bye? What if he flew off and didn't come back? she thought. What if the illusions he had about her were destroyed after one night of love?

"I need time," Sal said as he came up behind her, lifted her hair gently off her neck, and kissed her. His lips were warm and persuasive. Her spine tingled. She closed her eyes, head bowed forward as he moved his mouth around to the side of her neck.

"I know," he murmured with his teeth against her neck. "I know you do."

His hands swept lightly down the sides of her body and she was mesmerized by his gentle stroking. Very slowly he moved his palms up and down along the curves of her body. "I love you," he said.

Sal's lips parted in readiness. He brushed his lips lightly against hers, as if too much pressure would upset the delicate balance. His lips were full, dry, and warm as he tested hers. The reckless virility, the impatience she sensed in him was held masterfully in control. The result was an almost agonizing desire for him to seize her in his arms, to feel the fire of his spirit inflaming her. She knew that was what he wanted. That was what they both wanted.

"You're not running away," he teased her as he wrapped one arm around her body and pressed her against him. Her limbs seemed to weaken and fuse against his hard lean body. Very slowly he opened his mouth on hers. For so long now her passion had been reserved solely for her work, for her painting, for the future. But now she was in the present and the taste of Robert Capolla was sweeter than anything she might have imagined. There was nothing acquisitive or demanding. It was a kiss meant to reassure, to promise. He slipped his tongue inside her mouth with the same meticulous languor and began stroking in and out with a devastating gentleness that left her breathless and craving more.

"Is it too soon, Sal?" He drew her even closer and the rapid pounding of his heart against her tingling breast confirmed how tightly he was holding himself back.

He ran his tongue around her parted lips, and his dark eyes were smiling as he gazed at her. "You don't need to answer. I'm sleeping at the Boar's Head tonight, Sal . . . even if it does mean we'll both get a rotten night's sleep."

"You think you know everything about me." Sal cocked her head seductively to one side.

"I will soon." He licked playfully at her lips, then ran his tongue down to her chin, down the side of her long, slender neck, and back up to her ear. "You're going to think of me all week. By the time I arrive a week from this Saturday, I promise you won't have a doubt in your mind."

And he was right, Sal realized. Again! She felt a delicious agony to those intervening days, and although her schedule never deviated, she thought of him constantly. Whether she was lying in the stillness of her bed at night, painting down by the stream, or hauling fertilizer in her neighbors' old pickup, Robert Capolla seemed to possess her. How cunning of him, she thought. He must have known that his absence would dominate her perhaps even more than his presence.

He had suggested that she put in a phone so they could at least talk, but Sal had been firmly against it. Now it seemed that not hearing his voice actually intensified her yearning, and his letters, all ten of them, which had begun to arrive while he was still in London, more than compensated for the uneasy reality of most phone conversations.

Every afternoon Sal jogged down to the end of the lane, her heart pounding as she anticipated one of his cameo colored business envelopes with his office address embossed in the upper left corner: Robert C. Capolla Enterprises, Madison Avenue, New York City. His handwriting was surprisingly florid—curvy and exceptionally artistic and beautiful. Although he confessed in his first letter that writing was a task he seldom undertook, she sensed that he found pleasure in keeping her informed of his whereabouts and activities. The letters read almost like an intimate journal. Oddly, the absence of sexual innuendo made her longing for him even more intense.

The letters came by special carrier, and as if that weren't enough, there were bouquets of fresh flowers daily and on Friday, the day before he was due to arrive, a carton of saltines arrived.

"What's this all about?" Abe found Sal on her knees

71

in the middle of the kitchen floor, chuckling as she unpacked the enormous box of saltines.

"Some men give diamonds, others give saltines." Sal tossed Abe a box. "For Dorie and you, in lieu of champagne."

"I must say"—Abe sauntered on through—"I never would have figured Capolla for a sense of humor."

"Just because he's rich and handsome!" Sal shouted after him. "You're prejudiced!"

"Maybe so," Abe called back.

Saturday dawned bright and sunny. By noon the thermometer was hovering around one hundred. Sal forced herself to spend the afternoon down by the stream, painting, but her heart wasn't in it. It was as if she could feel his presence in the humid stillness. He was here, in Albemarle County—not in New York. The very idea of his proximity stirred her.

How amazing he was! she thought. He had seduced her from hundreds of miles away. Finally, she kicked off her sneakers, rolled up her jeans, and sat soaking her feet in the cool stream. She smiled, wriggling her toes under the water. Of course, she ruminated, he had known precisely what he was doing. No doubt he closed his business deals with the same imaginative cunning. And he had proved his point again by knowing that she would respond favorably to each carefully planned detail.

Despite all of her reservations about him, his lifestyle, his past with women, and his driving ambition, Sal had to admit that he fascinated her. His letters had given her an insight into him that might otherwise have taken her months to realize. In them she saw a man, not just driven by some egocentric desire to excel and build a vast empire, but impelled by certain principles of excellence; an idealist who truly believed that his contri-

72

bution could make the world a better place. He wrote specifically about his new automobile, explaining highly technical problems to her in such an articulate yet simple manner that she actually understood. The clarity of his thinking, coupled with his honest passion for his work, moved her. Most of the people she had come in contact with in the business world had a jaded outlook. Most felt that time-honored qualities such as moral integrity and passionate devotion to some idealistic goal were outmoded. Most prized coolness and sophistication above genuine excitement.

The letters also revealed a highly intellectual, eclectic spirit. Even with his hectic schedule in London, Robert had managed to attend a concert at Victoria and Albert Hall, and back in New York he had found an hour to take in a new art exhibit at the Whitney Museum.

Sal moved her legs back and forth in the cool stream, thinking that she probably was idealizing him. She smiled lazily, leaned back on her elbows and closed her eyes. But it was nice to idealize someone, she thought— to find someone who at least offered the possibility. Yes, she liked to think of Robert as a contemporary Thomas Jefferson, a man of rich and varied interests, a humanitarian, a gentleman. Jefferson, too, had loved inventions, and like Robert, he had been keenly interested in the scientific.

Now you're getting silly, she told herself as she pulled her legs out of the water and put on her sneakers. She was not given to such idle daydreaming, but today was an exception. Actually, in the ten days since she'd last seen him, she had painted like someone possessed. She would not go so far as to say he had inspired her, but somehow, thought that his passionately industrious spirit had affected her.

Sal lugged her equipment back toward the house,

73

weighing the pros and cons of their involvement. Since Sunday the pros had definitely outweighed the cons. Time was what they needed, she thought, and as far as she was concerned, they had all the time in the world—she was in no rush.

Abe was still painting when Sal finished dressing later that evening. She tiptoed into his studio and stood in the doorway, one hand poised on her hip, modeling the icy-blue sheath dress she had chosen for the occasion.

"Sexy." Abe nodded his approval. "I'm glad to see you took my advice, even if you didn't find poor ol' Leo quite to your liking."

"I like Leo." Sal moved nervously to the window and looked out.

"You didn't wear your blue sheath for him," Abe teased.

"What time is it?" Sal squinted.

"Eight. You haven't worn a dress in months."

"I've gained weight." Sal frowned, patting her well-rounded hips.

"You have not. I like your hair piled up on your head like that." Abe picked up his brush and began whistling under his breath as he painted.

"He should be here by now." Sal's palms were damp and she felt vaguely queasy.

She moved away from the window and stood indecisively in the middle of the room. "God, I hate this! I can't stand this waiting!"

"So put on your jeans and go back to work." Abe raised a malicious eyebrow. "Lock the door and draw the blinds and he'll never know you're here."

"Very funny." Sal gave him a wicked grin.

"Dorie is dying to meet him."

"Ummm." Sal waved her hand distractedly. She'd always hated this feeling. Maybe that was why she'd avoided men that really interested her all these years, she thought. She hated getting dressed up and waiting. It made her feel like someone about to be judged.

"When are you and Dorie getting married?"

"What brought that up?" Abe stopped painting abruptly.

"I don't know. . . ." Sal stared down at her feet. She'd spent at least an hour vacillating back and forth between heels and flats. Finally she'd chosen flats, thinking that Robert might be turned off if she was taller than he. Now she was irritated with herself for what seemed to be a niggardly compromise.

"Heels would look better." She looked up at Abe then back to her feet, as if they had been discussing footwear for some time.

"Sal." Abe eyed her fondly. "You're one of the most beautiful women I've ever known. I know you don't believe that, but trust me. I don't believe Capolla is going to spend the night looking at your feet. Frankly, I don't think he'd notice if you were eight feet tall."

"Some men do." Sal sighed.

"You've never worried about that," Abe reminded her.

"Well, I'm worried now, aren't I?" Sal's heart lurched at the sound of a car driving up the driveway.

"Don't worry," Abe called after her. "I won't be working all night. The house will be nicely deserted when you return with your prince in his golden coach."

Sal descended the staircase slowly, one hand on the banister, trying to catch her breath and ease the palpitations fluttering in her breast. As her footsteps echoed on the empty living room floor she heard the screen door slam in the kitchen.

The blue dress clung tightly to her voluptuous curves,

and with her hair piled on her head, she looked like a blond goddess moving gracefully through the darkness.

She paused as she entered the kitchen. The citrus aroma of his after-shave was like an aphrodisiac caressing her senses. For a moment she did not see him—the shadows had swallowed him up. She could only gaze in wonder at the magnificent bouquet of long-stemmed white roses which dominated the small kitchen table, transforming the old kitchen into an ethereal place. The moonlight spilled onto the table, giving the roses a shimmering, luminous quality that made them seem as alive as she felt.

Alive, so alive! He stepped out of the shadows. They stared through the murky darkness, sensing more than seeing each other. His white dinner jacket glowed, alive like the roses. Her image of the room was flooded with silvery moonlight; the roses and their two figures froze in her mind like a painting. She knew that one day she would paint this encounter between them.

He approached her slowly. "I missed you." His dark eyes searched her face hungrily.

"I missed you." Sal drank in the fine, chiseled angles of his handsome face.

"Jasmine. . . ." He brushed his lips lightly against her cheek, approving of her favorite perfume with a slight smile.

"I wondered what scent you'd wear," he murmured. "I like this. . . ."

He cradled her gently in his arms and Sal felt herself sinking into the rapturous bliss she had dreamed of for nearly a week—no, longer. She had dreamed of him holding her in his arms from the moment their eyes had met.

"It's hard to leave. . . ." He pulled away and stared at her. "Is this kitchen magic, or is it my imagination?"

Sal gave a low laugh. "Your roses certainly help. And the moonlight."

He shook his head. "No, it's more than roses and moonlight. Come. . . ."

He took her hand and guided her swiftly to the door. "A convertible!" Sal gasped at the sight of the sleek white car.

"I had a hell of a time renting a white convertible in Albemarle County. They had to drive this one down from Washington."

He opened the door and helped her into the front seat. "I'm a farmer." She threw back her head and laughed. All the nervousness was gone. Suddenly everything seemed wonderfully, excitingly hilarious.

"Look." She thrust her hand out to him as he sat behind the wheel. "I just want you to know for sure what you're gettin' into here. I washed and scrubbed the best I could but these are hardly—"

"I love your hands." Robert nibbled lightly on her fingertips. "They're working hands. My mother was a Sicilian farmer herself. Her hands looked a lot like yours."

"I'm Irish!" Sal joked as he shifted into first and drove smoothly down the lane. It was a perfect summer night, replete with a full moon and the thick heavy scent of honeysuckle in the air. Thinking of her panic earlier, she smiled—her indecision over which shoes to wear, her fear that somehow she had blown everything out of proportion and that when they faced each other again there would be only silence and awkwardness.

But there was no awkwardness, not even a moment's hesitation or ambivalence. The wind tore her carefully prepared hairdo to shreds and they both laughed as it flapped around to the front of her face, flying into her mouth and eyes.

77

"I feel like I'm going to the prom." Sal held her hands over her hair so she could talk. "I didn't know they made convertibles anymore."

"You're out of touch." Robert winked at her. "The automobile industry is into a whole new era of romance."

He slipped his arm along the seat and kneaded her shoulder gently with his fingers as he drove. Sal closed her eyes, feeling a wonderful, erotic drowsiness sweep over her. She rested her head on the back of the seat and gazed up at the stars, her heart quickening as his fingers grew more insistent. It felt so right being here beside him, with the warm wind rushing against her face.

"I didn't know they made nights like this anymore." Robert had reserved an outside table at an old inn overlooking Lake Ochiomo. He drew in a deep breath and reached for Sal's hand across the table.

For dinner they had shared a specially prepared stuffed pike poached in wine and delicately flavored with fresh tarragon. The bottle of champagne had been emptied long ago and now they sat smiling into each other's eyes, scarcely aware that they were the only diners left under the giant elm tree with its thick, gracefully dipping limbs.

"Dessert?" Robert's dark eyes twinkled suggestively and he nudged her knee under the table with his leg.

Sal held his eyes, a teasing smile curled at her lips, and she nudged him back under the table. "Yes, I'd love some. I've had my eye on those strawberry tarts all night. I hope they didn't run out."

Robert chuckled as he signaled the waiter. "Do you know I think you're the first woman I've been with in twenty years who's ordered dessert. All the women I know are obsessed with staying thin."

"Well, how can I turn down a strawberry tart?" Sal grinned at the waiter. "And lots of whipped cream, if you please."

"Yes, ma'am." The waiter cast her an admiring glance as he moved off toward the kitchen.

"It's relative." Sal turned back to Robert. "When I was keeping nine-to-five hours and indulging in all of those business lunches, I used to have to watch my step. But here, sometimes I forget to eat. It's like the air fills me, or maybe it's my involvement with painting. I don't know. Or maybe it just doesn't seem as important to worry about weight. Oh, sometimes I do, but mostly since I moved back to Virginia, to *your* farm, I just live. And, of course, in the summer, with all the fresh fruits and the tomatoes . . . Robert, you'll have to come with me and pick tomatoes, eat them fresh from the garden while they're still warm from the sun. Did you ever do that?"

"Never." Robert was watching her with a dreamy, relaxed expression. "When can we do that?"

"Tomorrow. . . ." Sal flushed, and suddenly her body was alive and throbbing with all that was implied in that word. Tomorrow they would be lovers.

Robert caught her eye. She knew he was thinking the same thing. She lowered her eyes, feeling suddenly shy, as if they were already standing naked in each other's presence. She had the distinct sense that he was reading her mind, that he had somehow seen into her past and knew that for a woman her age she was relatively inexperienced.

"You've always put all your energy into your business," he observed softly. "Is that it?"

"That's about it," Sal admitted as the waiter presented her with a strawberry tart heaped with freshly whipped cream. Sal stuck her finger in the cream and put a dab on her tongue.

"You're sure you don't want to indulge too?" She felt a deep thrill as she met Robert's bemused eyes.

"I'll watch." He folded his arms in front of his chest. "There's something of the voyeur in all of us, wouldn't you say?"

Sal sliced into the plump berries, making sure to create the perfect bite, which included just enough flaky crust and just the right amount of cream. His eyes were on her as she savored the bite. Her heart began to pound and wild sensations began to inflame her. She felt he was leading her through some dense erotic maze, toward a climax that was both desirable and terrifying.

She offered him a taste and he leaned across the table, opened his mouth, and took the sweet morsel inside. A dab of cream clung to the tip of his nose and Sal smiled at the incongruity of its presence on his clean-shaven face. She finished her tart with a smug little smile on her face and a giggle.

"Why are you laughing at me?" Robert's eyes darted mischievously in her direction.

Sal shook her head. Everything about him was so perfect, so dark and dashing, so sophisticated and suave, that the dab of unnoticed cream was making her hysterical. Well, nerves probably had something to do with it, she thought.

Deciding she couldn't very well let him summon the waiter and pay the bill with that big glob of cream on his nose, she beckoned to him with her forefinger and he bent his head toward her. "Robert . . . ?" Sal glanced furtively around the empty terrace, leaned forward, and licked the dab off the tip of his nose.

"Very nice." He touched his nose with an unruffled

smile. "Shall we dance with the others or go for a walk down by the lake?"

"The lake." Sal's eyes were glistening as he helped her out of her chair.

"Nice combo," he commented as they passed through the large room where a dozen or so couples were dancing to a mournful bluesy tune from the forties. "I wouldn't have thought they'd have such good music . . ."

". . . down here in the sticks!" Sal filled in, elbowing him lightly in the ribs. "You're such a snob, Robert Capolla. This is the south, home of rhythm and blues, home of some of the finest artists, poets, and writers. You're so busy jetting all over the world, you don't even know what's in your own backyard."

"I do now." Robert slipped his arm around her waist, and before she knew what was happening, he twirled her onto the dance floor. Sal caught her breath as his lean, hard body pressed into her soft curves. He was a brilliant dancer. She might have guessed as much, she thought, from the catlike energy he exuded when he walked. He held her tightly, yet his steps were graceful and flowing. She found herself gliding effortlessly around the dance floor, her own feet more sure, her body more in tune with the music than it had ever been. No, she had never been the dancing type—always a bit too tall, especially in her adolescence. Yet in Robert Capolla's arms she felt as lithe and graceful as a ballerina. For the first time in her life dancing was fun!

His warm breath on her neck sent delicious tremors along her spine, and when he tightened his grip on her hand she responded, squeezing his and snuggling closer. She closed her eyes and sank against his chest, allowing him to steer her, feeling only the throb of his heart, hearing only the sexy trombone crooning its song. His hand strayed briefly to the curve of her hip, and she felt his longing and his restraint in his quick intake of breath.

Still they danced on and on, as if they were already enmeshed in an erotic tangle and could not escape for a moment. Even when the music turned fast and the combo blasted out some current rock tune, they still could not leave. They danced to the raucous music, flushed and damp, their eyes glittering with excitement. The dancing was propelling them headlong into an erotic fervor that left them both breathless.

"You said it. . . ." Robert turned to her when they were seated in the convertible about to drive home. "You said it felt like we were going to a prom. I haven't danced like that—"

He broke off and gave her a quiet, searching look, then turned on the ignition. They drove home in utter silence, drinking in the night air, watching the sky throb white with heat lightning. As they turned up the lane, a quiver of nervousness threatened to ruin the absolute perfection of the evening.

Robert reached out and took her hand. How could he have felt her hesitation? Yet he seemed to have known the very instant she was besieged with doubt.

He held her hand securely until the car stopped, then drew her close and pressed his mouth against hers. She felt malleable, like eager clay giving in to the tenderness of his touch as he stroked her neck and traced one finger down between the damp cleavage of her breasts.

"I want you so!" The deep moan seemed torn from him. A chill of apprehension swept over her. She had never heard, nor felt, so much passion from any other living soul.

CHAPTER FIVE

They moved through the house like two ghosts, hand in hand in the shimmering shadows. The heat lightning, silent and ghostlike, too, filled the house with splashes of unexpected white light as Sal led the way up the sagging staircase to her room.

Her room, his house. Earlier in the evening they had joked about him being her landlord and about the abysmal way she kept house. Now it seemed that their evening together, the laughter, conversation, the dancing and the wind in her hair, existed in some distant past. As they crossed the threshold into her bedroom it felt as if they had journeyed long and far to arrive at just this point. In her heart she felt she had known Robert Capolla forever.

"I've ached for this moment from the instant I laid eyes on you." Robert held her at arm's length. Slowly his eyes traveled the length of her tall sturdy body and returned to gaze deeply into her eyes.

"It's not too soon now, is it, Sal?" The intensity of his desire rumbled in his voice.

"It's nice of you to ask. . . ." Sal felt herself irresistibly drawn to him. She knew precisely what she was doing. Somehow, Robert had known she would want it that way.

Robert gave a low moan as he pressed against her, his hands spread fanlike over her behind as he tilted her body into his.

"Sal!" His mouth, so fierce and yet so gentle, opened onto hers and she yielded, parting her lips, almost panting for the slow deliberate entry of his quick-fire tongue.

Suddenly his hands seemed to be everywhere at once. She felt dizzy and wondered how she remained standing as he unzipped her dress, drew it over her head, unhooked her bra, and clasped her large firm breasts, one in each hand.

His eyes were glazed as he stared at her breasts, which were pale and white in contrast to her deeply tanned arms and shoulders. He placed her hand on his belt and she felt the pulsating heat which radiated from the depths of his virility. As his hands skimmed the contours of her naked torso, she unbuckled his belt and, scarcely breathing, slipped her hands onto the cool bare skin of his hips. The sensations of her hands on his bare flesh propelled him into an uncontrollable fever.

"I'm sorry, Sal . . . I've been waiting too long for this!" In a blur he removed his clothes and lowered her onto the bed.

His body was hot with passion. He was lean, tight, and seemed entirely constructed of smooth, flawless muscle. He gently fell on top of her, a gratifying weight that made her moan in ecstasy. He kissed her wildly, his tongue like the devil's own spear hurled into her. She dug her fingers into his shoulders as she kissed him back with an abandoned intensity that startled her.

She wondered how he had seen that part of her she kept to herself, obscured beneath the image of plain-spoken, easygoing Sal.

His flanks were silky smooth, as soft and fine as hers. Sal searched along his back with her hands as his mouth covered one breast and his tongue drew damp circles around her large rosy nipple. He pushed his chin against her voluptuous breast and blew a stream of hot air against her other nipple, till she was nearly mad with longing.

"I could make love to you all night, Sal," he murmured. "But first . . ."

His breath was coming in hoarse, ragged gasps, and his gaze held hers as he drew off the final barrier, her sheer white panties. Bending over her, he stared down at her body.

Sal reached up to him. The flames which licked and curled inside were almost too painful to bear. Small cataclysms, warm and deliciously promising, were already breaking inside her. Just his eyes, as they feasted on her smooth stomach and drank in the wonder of her femininity, were enough to inflame her.

He ran one hand across her taut stomach, and still crouching over her as if he were about to spring, he petted her lower and lower, until he reached his mark. The pressure of his hand brought forth a rush of hot sensations. She closed her eyes, twisting in ecstasy as he bent his head and kissed her where his hand had rested briefly.

She was so ready that she thought one more moment's delay would be unbearable. The pleasure offered by the light kisses he dropped along her inner thigh was almost unendurable. She gasped and ran her hands through his thick dark hair.

"Ah, Sal. . . ." He parted her legs with his hands, and although she could not see him, she could feel his eyes drinking in all her beauty. He touched her lightly with one finger and she arched upwards, mad for more.

"Yes . . . now." He moved decisively, and in one smooth stroke he filled her.

"Robert!" she cried out, arching up, turning her head from side to side on the pillow. Waves of erotic frenzy broke inside of her, sending hot currents through her entire body. She was laughing now, staring into his dark eyes, meeting his thrusts, anticipating his next move as if they were one.

Yes, she felt they were one mind, one body, linked together in a way that she never wanted to end; and she knew, by the determined look that crossed his face from time to time, that he too desired their time together to go on and on forever.

"I love you." He breathed the words in rhythm with his heaving body. Sal drew in a deep breath, readying herself for the next surge of passion. His mouth clung to hers, soft and insistent.

Yes, he was a man of many colors, many temperaments. His lovemaking was wild and violent, yet almost miraculously tempered by sudden unexpected gentle intervals.

"I love you," he whispered again into her ear. She wondered if it could be true.

The next morning Sal woke on cue at her usual hour without the benefit of the aroma of coffee. She blinked at the sleeping body next to her, smiled, stretched her arm out instinctively to touch his cheek, then pulled back. She'd be willing to bet that Robert Capolla was not an early riser. Probably it had been years since he had awakened at five A.M. She rolled onto her side and studied his sleeping profile, so handsome, so serene. Just looking at him made her pulse race. Now, she thought, they had so many memories. . . .

She drew in a cautious, steadying breath as her mind swept rapidly over each delicious detail of last night— the roses, the car, the laughter, the conversation, the dancing, and finally, their lovemaking.

Once again her hand was drawn to his cheek, as if the impulse to caress him was just too strong. Love? A tiny frown creased the invisible line between her pale eyebrows. He seemed so at home saying the word. No, she couldn't really take it seriously, could she? She knew that some people were like that. Some people, both men and women from what she could determine, just had to say "I love you." And maybe they meant it at the time. Certainly, she didn't hold it against him. But he couldn't love her. It was too soon for that, wasn't it?

She smiled, feeling expansive, excited, and vigorously energetic. It touched her that he'd said "I love you," even if he'd meant it only for the moment. She, on the other hand, was a person who withheld words, especially emotionally charged words like love. She had never said "I love you" . . . not even to the man she had been involved with her last year of college, the only man who had even made the word leap to the forefront of her mind. And of all the men she had dated in Chicago, not one of them had prompted her to think in terms of love, in terms of permanence.

But that's the way she was, she mused—so different from Robert. Love? She rolled onto her other side and stared out the window through the leafy mass of sycamore leaves to the rich green lawn, sparkling with dew from last night's downpour. She hadn't even heard the rain, could only remember the flashes of heat lightning and then . . .

She felt like laughing. Her body was shot with adrenaline. Minutes later she was fully dressed, humming to herself as she put on a full pot of coffee. They would have the entire day, she thought, and Robert had hinted last night that he might change a business meeting and take an early Monday flight back to New York, so he could stay over. Bubbles of warm, remembered pleasure broke inside her body as she went about her chores. Her daily routine felt entirely new. Everywhere she looked the world shimmered with new light, as if the place had been charmed overnight.

"Well, it has!" Sal grinned as she picked the last of the newly ripened tomatoes. She stacked the small cartons of freshly picked vegetables in the back of her car and drove down to the little shack at the foot of the lane. Sunday was a big day at the vegetable stand. During the week, when mostly local people patronized the stand, she left the stand unattended, leaving a big Mason jar where people could drop money and relying on the honor system. But on Saturdays and Sundays, Wendell tended shop.

As she drove back up the driveway, she scrutinized the old house for signs of life. Inside it was quiet. She could visualize his sleeping body, but just to be sure, she tiptoed upstairs and peeked in at him.

She grinned, grabbed her robe and a pair of clean jeans and a shirt. He was still in the same position. She resisted the urge to make a racket that would wake him.

After her shower, her face shining, her hair wet and skimmed back from her face and knotted with a rubber band, Sal looked in on him again. How could anyone sleep so late? she wondered. It was nearly ten o'clock and the stifling valley heat was already supplanting the early morning sweetness. He'd missed the best part of the day, she thought.

Sal opened her mouth to call to him, but decided to wait. She had almost forgotten what it was like to sleep like that—like a city person. She had done exactly the same thing during her years as a businesswoman in Chicago. By the time Sunday rolled around she had invariably been so exhausted that often she'd spent the entire day in bed. Now she was so in tune with the changing patterns of light and the sounds of nature, that she couldn't imagine staying in bed even until nine.

Sal slipped into her studio and lost herself in fleshing out some of the details on her painting. She wouldn't get down to the stream today but on Monday, she decided, after Robert was gone, she would spend the whole afternoon there. Perhaps she would even finish this painting and start another one. The next time Robert came down she would have something to show him. Sal smiled. He really was good for her!

She lost track of the time, and when she glanced at the sad-looking Big Ben clock she and Abe had retrieved from the local dump, its stubby broken hour hand was resting on twelve. Sal dropped her brush and ran down to the hall to her bedroom.

"Damn!" He was gone, already up for Lord only knew how long. She raced toward the stairs.

How could she have been so careless? she asked herself. Their minutes together were precious. She'd never imagined herself spending the entire morning painting. She'd been certain they would both end up back in her bed, laughing, making love in broad daylight.

"Sorry." She gave him a rueful smile as she entered the kitchen. He was seated at the kitchen table, dressed, shaved, and sipping his coffee with a detached expression.

She sat down across from him and gave him a hopeful smile.

"I see you found the coffee." Sal felt suddenly shy in his presence. She looked down at her bare feet. The contrast between them was overwhelming.

"And the orange juice." Robert lifted his empty glass.

"I have eggs too."

Robert shook his head. "No eggs for me. So . . . you were up bright and early, I see."

"I think I'll have some more coffee." Sal moved to the counter. With her back to him she stared out into the glaring noonday sun, feeling his eyes on her. He was dressed casually in a pair of crisp white trousers, a white and yellow T-shirt stretched tautly across his broad chest. He was wearing Top-Siders without socks. He looked, for the first time, ill-at-ease. He would have been more comfortable, she thought, on the prow of a yacht, sailing around the French Riviera.

"I always wake between five and five thirty," she said as she returned to the table.

"I would have thought you might have slept a bit more soundly than usual." He gave her an unruffled smile.

Sal's eyes widened in astonishment. Was it possible his feelings were hurt? That he felt somehow threatened because she had gone about her business as usual?

"Chickens can't wait till noon, Robert," she said. "And I had a bushel of tomatoes to pick."

"You should have help," he said with the same unruffled smile.

Sal's stomach tightened. She'd always known he was used to giving orders, but she didn't like his tone. It was his farm, that was true, but she was running it. "I do have help. Two high school boys work for me during the week. Sunday's their day off. Except Wendell takes care of the stand."

"I would think you'd need more help on weekends. Isn't that when you do the biggest business at the stand?"

"Maybe so." Sal wondered why she resented his suggestion.

"You'll have to make other arrangements after they return to school in September," Robert said.

"I know it." Sal felt suddenly uneasy. Why was he going on about the stand and her hired help? What was he really thinking? "Do you want some more coffee, Robert?" she asked.

"No thanks. I've had three cups." His eyes were guarded.

Sal shrugged, wishing she could make light of his moodiness. Suddenly everything had turned so damn serious. He was annoyed with her for getting up early and losing track of the time, and now she was annoyed with him for encroaching on her turf. She glanced at the white roses, half expecting to find them drooping and yellowed. But, no, they at least showed no sign that the magic of their romance was on the wane.

"Robert, we seem to be on the verge of an argument and I don't know . . ." Sal gave him a candid look which was tinged with regret.

"I couldn't figure out where you'd gone." He looked past her, as if something interested him outside. "You weren't in the barn, or in the garden."

"I'm sorry." Sal shifted uncomfortably in her chair. "I didn't want to disturb you. You seemed so greedy for your sleep. I remember how that used to feel. Sunday was always a day to catch up. Now Sunday is a day to do more things, to relax, swim, go visiting."

"A kiss on the cheek wouldn't have disturbed me."
Robert looked at her slowly.

Sal nodded reluctantly. In a way, he was right. Still, it bothered her that he needed her to apologize, again. She'd already said she was sorry once. She sipped her coffee, debating about confronting the real issue head on. It was obvious to her that Robert was not accustomed to an independent woman who would crawl out of bed on her own and go about her business. She had hurt his ego and now he was trying to pin all of the responsibility on her.

On the other hand, what was the point in making a mountain out of a molehill when they were just getting to know one another? Wasn't it just a sign of his caring?

"I'll flip you for the day's activities." Sal dug in her pocket and came out with a quarter.

Robert gave her a long hard look, then smiled suddenly, clasping her hand. "Don't disappear again, okay?"

"I promise." Sal's heart quickened as he leaned across the table and kissed her.

He ran his tongue around her lips, tasting her, and she could feel him relishing his memories of their intimacy. He flicked his tongue inside her mouth and she welcomed him, yearning toward him across the table.

"You sure you don't want to go back to bed?" Robert's lips were warm and coaxing.

"Of course that's what I want!" Sal's breasts seemed to bloom as he reached over and covered them with his hands.

Two hours later they walked outside, euphoric and relaxed, oblivious to the skyrocketing temperature. They had spent the last hour frolicking in Sal's unreliable shower, and Robert was insisting that he was going to order extensive renovations to begin on Monday.

"Good luck," Sal told him as she put on a pair of large, round dark glasses and pulled a straw hat snugly over her damp hair. "You will be performing a miracle if you get a plumber here before winter."

"I like a challenge." Robert pinched her lightly on the rear end as she climbed into the convertible.

"You're so smug," Sal teased. "Don't be too smug, Robert, just because you won that flip. I'll get you backpacking yet."

Robert chuckled to himself and darted devilish looks at her as they wound around the steep curves on their way to visit Thomas Jefferson's Monticello.

"Backpacking." He shook his head, smiling. "It's so hot you can hardly breathe, and you want to go backpacking, hiking up mountains with thermoses full of beer and soggy bologna sandwiches on our back."

"I can't believe you've never once been on a hike." Sal moved closer to him in the front seat of the convertible.

"Would I lie about a thing like that?" He cast her a sideways glance.

"Okay." Sal narrowed her eyes against the wind which whipped past them as they came to a straightaway and Robert accelerated the car. "Like I said, smartie, you won the toss today. We're going to Monticello because you won, that's what you wanted. I'm a good loser. But stand warned—this is not going to set the precedent. You are not going to win all the flips!"

Robert hugged her close as he guided the car with one expert hand. "You won't blame me if I try though, will you?"

Although Sal had toured Monticello from the time she was a child in grade school, seeing it through Robert's eyes made the experience seem utterly new. Located on a mountaintop, the house, an architectural masterpiece, surveyĕd the rolling Virginia countryside Jefferson loved so well.

"What a man," Robert said as he stood in awe beneath the famous seven-day clock in the entrance hall. Throughout the house there were reminders of Jefferson's creative mind, his interest in science and attention to aesthetic detail.

"I'm always struck by the simplicity." Sal laced her fingers through Robert's. "By how modern and contemporary it feels."

"I could live in a house like this." Robert looked admiringly over his shoulder as they walked outside and entered the garden, also designed by Jefferson.

"I'll bet you could!" Sal laughed. She thought again of how much Robert reminded her of Thomas Jefferson. Not only was he a man of many facets—highly intellectual and with a fascination for science and a deep appreciation for beauty—he also possessed an elegance that made him look at home in such royal surroundings.

"What I mean," Robert went on as they strolled along the meandering roundabout walk on the west lawn, "is that I could really live in a place like this. Forever, as a home. That's something I've never had, something I haven't given much thought to. My homes are always made for me. They were necessary details which were attended to by others—first my mother and father and then my wives. Until I saw this place, I never really knew what a home could mean to someone. Obviously it meant a great deal to Thomas Jefferson."

"Yes." Sal veered off the path to sit beneath a giant magnolia tree. She spread her pale-blue cotton skirt around her, removed her straw hat, and stretched her long legs in front of her. Robert seemed at home here in the shadow of such aristocratic surroundings, but she wasn't sure about herself.

She cast a disapproving glance at her bare feet. She had automatically slipped out of her sandals before sitting down on the velvety green lawn. Robert sat next to her, looking back toward the mansion with a pensive expression. He looked elegant and cool, more handsome than she had ever seen him, perhaps because he looked so serene.

And what about her? she wondered. She tucked her bare feet under her and clasped her hands tightly in her lap. Suddenly she was overwhelmed by reasons why things could never work out between them. Robert dined with princes, for heaven's sake! And when he was in London he'd had lunch with the Prime Minister, to discuss the possibility of more British financial backing for his automobiles.

She wasn't shy about meeting the Prime Minister or Saudi oil moguls. That wasn't it, she thought. She would no doubt find them just as likeable or unlikeable as the citizens of Blue Mills. It was that she had left that busy-busy world behind. She had never really enjoyed business cocktail parties, and she knew that was largely what Robert's life consisted of: endless parties, endless obligations, tight schedules that would leave her no time to paint. She knew she could never go back to that life.

She was an artist. She had shed her suits and silk shirts for stained jeans. She preferred her feet bare, and upon leaving Chicago had promised herself she would never make another list of things to do. Her life was full now without being crammed.

She was an artist, and he was a businessman. His business was putting deals together, raising money, making connections, matching, juggling, flying here and there—presenting his case to the world. He was a man on the move. Movement was the essence of who he was. And she wanted stillness.

She wanted peace and quiet and time; time to allow her artistic ideas to ferment, time to experiment artistically and take chances.

"What is it?" Robert turned back to her with concerned eyes.

Sal shook her head dismissing him, but he took her hand and held it. "You're the most beautiful woman I've ever known," he said softly.

"Robert . . ." She shook her head again. His compliments made her uneasy.

"Didn't you notice people staring at you inside?"

"No."

"You're sure you're not pretending to be modest?" he joshed lightly.

"I'm pretty sure," Sal drawled, "I'm not ugly."

"How about beautiful?" He increased the pressure on her hand and she felt her heart beat faster.

"I don't think about it." She smiled.

"You're the Venus . . . Diana the Huntress, some exotic Amazon queen."

"And you're a fruitcake." Sal flushed, her worries utterly dispelled. "The one thing I've noticed is that I am a little less gawky since I turned thirty."

"You're a woman," Robert observed, "who grows more beautiful with time. Why don't you fly to New York with me tomorrow?"

"What?" Sal practically bolted to her feet. Robert held her arm insistently.

"It's supposed to be in the hundreds here every day next week. You've been working your gorgeous butt off all summer. Take a week off. Enjoy the air conditioning on Park Avenue. We'll go to the theater, art galleries. I know it makes you nervous when I talk about helping you find a gallery, but at least I could introduce you to that lawyer I told you about and to a couple of friends of mine who own galleries. I promise not to be pushy. Besides, you might be impressed with my own art collection. It might prove that I am not entirely without an aesthetic eye myself!"

Sal laughed despite her uneasiness. "You win the Renaissance Man award of the year."

"I'll make a light work week for myself," Robert went on, heartened by her response. "I have to fly to Detroit early Wednesday, but I'll be back in time for supper. Besides, you'll need a day off from me by then . . . knowing you. And don't tell me you'll miss your painting. We'll bring whatever you need along. You can set up your easel in the room my kids stay in when they come for visits. I'll leave the car at your disposal, you can go anyplace you want. . . ."

"Robert . . ." Sal placed a restraining hand over his mouth. Determination sparked in his dark eyes, and she felt herself wavering.

"Robert, what about my tomatoes? What about three fields of corn about to be harvested? Two cows are about to deliver, what about them? Not to mention a zillion other details. There's no way I can just drop everything and fly up—"

"You can do anything if you want to," Robert interrupted persuasively. "You above all people know that's true, Sal."

Sal paused. He had her there. That was precisely the belief she subscribed to. "Then . . . I guess I don't want to go to New York."

For a moment he looked totally flabbergasted, stung by the honesty of her retort. "I guess I asked for that," he said archly. "Never ask Sal Carter a straight question if you don't want a straight answer."

"Robert, I just left the city. True, it wasn't New York and . . ."

". . . and you could go to a lot of art galleries. New York is the art center of the world. You as an aspiring artist should look around and see what sort of competition you have."

"I'm not in competition." Sal felt suddenly overwhelmed by his arguments. He was a man who did not give up easily, a man who did not take no for an answer.

Sal rallied her fighting spirit. "Summer is a bad time," she said. After all, she was not exactly a novice at the art of winning her point. "It's coming on to harvest time. Use your head, Robert." She smiled at him. "A farmer doesn't leave the farm at the peak of the season. Besides, air conditioning makes me sneeze. My eyes will swell up and you won't like looking at me."

Robert chuckled as he regarded her. "I'll flip you for it." He reached into his pocket for a quarter. "Heads you come to New York—"

"No." She reached for the quarter and without the slightest hesitation heaved it over her shoulder. "We don't flip for everything, Robert."

A momentary look of consternation crossed his face, and for an instant Sal wondered if he wasn't going to react badly. But then he smiled and lay down on the grass with his head in her lap.

"Well, well," he said softly as he smiled up at the blue sky. "It looks like I'm going to be seeing a lot of the Shenandoah Valley this summer."

CHAPTER SIX

The next six weekends were a blur of summer heat, laughter, and dazzling forays into a scintillating erotica never before experienced or ever even dreamed of by Sal Carter. Once a week, on Friday, Robert chartered a private plane to bring him down, and Sal met him at the Charlottesville airport. While Robert was there, he picked tomatoes and fed the chickens, among other things, and on several occasions filled in down at the stand for an ailing Wendell. Usually he left early Monday morning, though once he lingered until Tuesday.

However, after the first torrid month Sal began to stagger through Mondays, bleary-eyed from taking advantage of every moment of Robert's visit. It was finally dawning on her that Mondays were lost. That left Tuesdays, Wednesdays, and Thursdays to paint. Usually, by the time Friday rolled around, she was either uncertain about Robert's arrival time or too excited about seeing him again to really lose herself in her art work. Vaguely it occurred to her that the summer was slipping away and that her plan to have a substantial amount of work completed by autumn was almost an impossibility.

For the first time since her initial reservations about him, Sal was uneasy. She peered begrudgingly into Abe's studio. He was too engrossed in his painting to even notice her. Abe's discipline was paying off. He had completed a dozen new paintings since spring and was slated to have a show at the university in October. Well, she thought, at least someone had spent a diligent and productive summer.

Sal frowned and slumped along the narrow upstairs corridor to the bathroom. Mel O'Sullivan, who ran the small gallery at the university, had been as interested in her work as he had been in Abe's. If she hadn't frittered away an entire summer, she would be having a show too.

She entered the gleaming white-tiled bathroom and regarded her wilted image in the mirror which was ringed with small light bulbs. True to his word, Robert had ordered a complete renovation of the bathroom, installing the best Italian white tiles, a custom made Jacuzzi, and expanding the small window so that the blue Shenandoah Mountains were now visible. Workmen had appeared as if by magic and the entire job had miraculously been completed in less than a week. When Robert flew down the weekend following the renovation, he presented Sal with a box from Bloomingdale's filled with luxurious white Turkish towels, a plethora of jasmine-scented soap, an array of exotic oils, and a sexy white silk robe.

The bathroom was flashy, ultra-modern, and totally out of keeping with the crumbling antebellum mansion. But somehow it was right, and every time she gazed out the newly enlarged window at the purple range in the west, she thought of Robert and her heart bloomed. But she still wasn't willing to call it love. Usually, she avoided analyzing her feelings where he was concerned. When she did give into introspection, the word that seemed to suit her feelings best was *fascination*.

Robert Capolla fascinated her. The more she knew him, the more he fascinated her. Lately, she could scarcely think of anything else. Lately, even Tuesdays, Wednesdays, and Thursdays were becoming a blur.

Sal stripped out of her dusty overalls, and after removing her underwear, stepped under a steaming shower. Her body ached with a familiar fatigue—not a clean ache, but a heavy, dull, deadening fatigue, the sort she used to experience back in Chicago.

Where was it all leading? she wondered. Now that a few leaves were browning around the edges and there were fewer blossoms on the tomato plants, her mind was drawn to winter—to the future.

Sal stepped out of the shower and wrapped her body in one of Robert's enormous nubby white towels. It was unusual for her to avoid looking at reality squarely, but now she realized that was precisely what she'd been doing. The reason her painting had fallen by the wayside was because Robert's weekends were long and getting longer, and because it perturbed him when she took time away from him to go into her studio.

She reached for the silk robe he had given her, thought better of it, and pulled on her ratty old blue terry-cloth robe with the torn sleeve. She tied the robe irritably. It was nobody's fault but her own, she thought. She'd been rationalizing all along that since he flew all the way down, it was unfair of her to spend even an hour painting.

She padded back out into the hall as the phone rang. That was another thing Robert had miraculously provided, insisting that if they had to be separated, the least

Sal could do was to allow him to have a phone installed. And so there were now four phones in the house: one in her bedroom, one in her main studio, one in the kitchen, and a cordless phone for when she was out "shooting the bull with the cows," as Robert joked.

"Hello," Sal drawled, trying not to sound too depressed, in case it was her elderly friend Martha, who had a knack for reading her mind.

"Good news." It was Robert, and she could tell he was excited. "I don't have to fly to London after all. A Japanese company is going to invest. We just closed the deal."

"That's wonderful." Sal tried to dredge up some genuine enthusiasm. She knew he'd been worried about raising additional outside funds to finance his car. Business had been rather rough for him lately. There was a lot of public criticism, a lot of skepticism about the validity of his current automotive project.

"This means we can continue the research I told you about last week. It means that with any luck at all we can go into production within the next two years!"

"Congratulations!" Sal smiled, for her own benefit. She was glad Robert wasn't here. Like Martha Gross, he could read her every thought. But then, she'd never been a good faker.

"And . . ." he paused melodramatically, "all of this means that I can leave tonight."

"It's Wednesday!" Sal could not disguise her alarm.

"Have you eaten dinner?" Robert rushed on. "I can be in Charlottesville in time to eat with you."

Sal shook her head, disgruntled, disoriented by the news. He was coming down tonight? And she'd just been revving up to put in some long hours at the easel on Thursday, and maybe even Friday morning.

"Robert . . ." She tried for the third time to inter-

102

rupt his enthusiastic plan to fly down with fresh lobster and champagne so they could celebrate.

"Robert . . . it's no good if you come down tonight." Her statement hung in the empty silence of the long distance connection.

"You have plans . . . ?" There was a note of disbelief in his voice.

"No, no, no." Sal's tone, usually so calm and placid, was distorted with a frenetic urgency. She had to make him understand! "It's just that I'd planned on working late tonight . . . painting. I thought I might even paint all night if things went well. I haven't done that in . . . well, not in a long time, Robert, and today I just started gettin' a bit down about how lax I've been."

"You're blaming me, aren't you?"

"No, no, I'm not! Not really . . ." Sal tensed as she waited for him to say something.

"I've been through this kind of thing before, Sal." He sounded bitter, almost mean. "You're telling me it's my fault because you haven't been painting."

Sal's cheeks grew hot at the hostility in his voice, and for the moment she lost sight of what was really happening. "You make it very hard, Robert." She clutched the receiver until her knuckles turned white.

"The truth is, I can't leave you alone when you come down. You don't even like it when I get up before you to feed the chickens. But you understand the chickens are living, breathing creatures. They would die without feed. My canvas, on the other hand, could stand blank in my studio for an eternity and not suffer at all from malnutrition."

"I had no idea you were harboring such resentment," he said tightly after another long pause. "I've tried to help . . . with the damn chickens, the damn tomatoes, and—"

103

"I know, I know," Sal jumped in. "You're sensitive to the chores. I know you've tried. And spending three hours on Sunday at the stand. . . . I'm sorry! It came out all wrong."

"I just closed a very big deal," he said emphatically, as if she must have misunderstood his excitement.

"I know." Sal slumped against the wall in exasperation.

"Well, happy painting. I'll have to find some other way to celebrate."

"Robert!" Sal stared at the receiver as the line went dead. She stood there numb, with a sense of unreality about what had happened. She waited for the phone to ring again, for him to laugh and say yes, he really understood. She dialed his apartment, knowing he wouldn't be there because he must have been calling from wherever his business meeting was. There was no answer—the housekeeper wasn't even there to take a message. Sal paced anxiously into her bedroom, folded her arms, and sat on the edge of the bed. He would call back because he would know she couldn't reach him, because he would know that she already regretted everything that had been said. Of course she wanted him to come down and celebrate! Why had she been so shortsighted?

She dialed information and got his office number, but then just as it started to ring she hung up. Did she really want him to come down?

She stared at the fancy white push-button phone he had purchased for the bedroom. The phone wasn't her. For an instant she wanted to yank it out of the wall and hurl it out the window. This entire misunderstanding never would have happened if it hadn't been for the damn phone! she thought.

Her heart was pounding now, and the longer she

waited for the phone to ring, the harder it pounded. What if he never phoned again? she wondered. What if this was the end?

The thought caught her up short. It was as if some invisible icy hands were trying to strangle her. She grabbed the phone and dialed his office.

"Sorry, Mr. Capolla and his staff have left for the day. This is his answering service."

Sal sank back onto her bed and stared out the window as the last purple streaks faded to black. What would it be like to be married to him? Oh, she knew the answer to that, but she'd been ignoring it. Robert was wonderful, generous beyond imagining—only he wanted things his way. *Always*. Usually he could manage a joke, a charming smile, or some witticism to lend an air of moderation to his determination. He had none of the obvious, distasteful flaws of a tyrant.

Sal closed her eyes, praying that she would fall asleep so the pain would stop. Robert would, of course, say that he encouraged her painting. And it was true that he lauded her, she admitted, heaped praise on everything she showed him. She had no doubt that he would introduce her to the most powerful impresarios in the art world if she would allow him. He would go to any extreme, she knew, to catapult her into the foreground of the New York art scene. He would do all this, but he could not tolerate the time her painting took from him.

She watched the hands of the clock creep toward nine, and finally she dragged herself out of bed and went back into Abe's studio. He was cleaning his brushes and had that excited flush that sometimes occurs after a particularly good day's work.

"You look awful." Abe regarded her solemnly.

"I think I just blew things between Robert and me."

105

Sal crossed over to one of three rickety chairs Abe had recently salvaged from the dump.

"Just like that?" Abe looked skeptical.

"On the damned phone!" Sal scowled.

"Want to tell me?" Abe sat down and folded his paint-stained hands as Sal described the unfortunate phone conversation.

"He just needs time to cool off," Abe offered. "You bruised his ego. He's not used to being told no."

"I know." Sal felt like crying. How could she love a man like Robert Capolla? she wondered. A domineering, basically old-fashioned—Her mouth dropped suddenly. Love? Was she finally admitting it to herself?

"How did you know Robert likes having his own way?" Sal looked back at Abe. "You've only met him once."

"I read too." Abe nudged her lightly on the knee. "Anyway, even if I hadn't read all that press on Capolla, I would have known by looking at him. Does the word arrogant seem too harsh?"

"But that's not all there is to him!" Sal sprang to Robert's defense.

"Of course not." Abe gave her a sympathetic smile. "No one is just one thing. But, Sal, a woman like you, so independent, so determined to do it all yourself . . . I just haven't been able to figure you and Capolla out. I'm not saying he's a scoundrel or—"

"Anyway"—Sal shook her head as if she were about to dismiss the subject—"it's just been a lark."

"You're not exactly the 'lark' sort," Abe said.

"But I knew it would be just a brief sort of affair. I mean, I'm not that naive, Abe."

Abe nodded understandingly, but Sal looked away. She hadn't fooled him. They both knew that things between her and Robert had gone a bit further than a casual summer romance . . . at least for her.

"Why don't you get dressed," Abe suggested. "We'll drive into Charlottesville and I'll take you to that country-western place I was telling you about."

"What about Dorie?" Sal asked automatically, her mind still reeling from its recent acknowledgment of love.

"Dorie and I take Wednesday nights off from each other." Abe winked. "She's very secretive, but I think she's taking a carpentry class because lately her fingers are full of little slivers."

Sal gave a wry laugh. "You and Dorie are some pair."

"Get dressed." Abe pulled her to her feet and Sal shuffled back into her bedroom, threw on a pair of brown linen slacks, a beige shirt, and sandals. Thank heavens for Abe, she thought. She couldn't imagine spending the evening alone. She'd rip the phone out if she had to stare at it all night!

"Tomorrow I'm calling the phone company," she said aloud. "They can just come and remove those instruments of the devil."

Several hours later Sal sat hunched over her beer in the dimly lit Depot Bar and Grill. The music had helped for a while, especially when it was fast, with a lot of intricate fiddle pickin'. But the last song, before the trio took their break, had been a weepy country blues number, and now she was feeling the pain all over again.

"Sal, why don't you try to call him again if you're so upset?" Abe took her hand and gave her an encouraging smile.

"I tried his apartment the last time I went to the ladies' room," Sal confessed guiltily. "It's nearly midnight."

"So maybe he's out drowning his sorrows like you are."

"Ha!" Sal raised a sarcastic eyebrow and downed the rest of her beer. She'd never been much of a drinker and tonight had exceeded her limit by several beers. And then she hadn't been able to eat her hamburger, despite Abe's badgering.

"Not Robert Capolla! No, he's not the type to drown his sorrows. Certainly not in beer. Too plebeian. No, Robert's idea of dealing with pain and disappointment is to move on . . . to buy up another company, close another business deal, seduce someone new—"

"Sal, if you feel that way about him, how can you be so upset? Maybe it's good riddance, if that's the kind of man he is."

"What do you think?" Sal asked, studying Abe.

"It doesn't matter what I think," Abe said reluctantly.

"Tell me," Sal pressured. "Abe, you've known me almost all my life. Have I been a fool? You may as well tell me now. I couldn't feel any worse than I do."

"No, you haven't been a fool." Abe signaled their waiter for a check.

"One more," Sal pleaded. "Just one."

"Okay." Abe held up two fingers as the waiter headed toward them.

"Tell me what you think," Sal persisted.

"For one thing, I think you're blowing your argument with Robert out of proportion. I don't understand quite why. It's not like you. For another, I think you were particularly vulnerable when Capolla came into your life two months ago. You allowed him to sweep you off your feet . . . something you wouldn't have done if you'd been behind a desk or met him at one of those cocktail parties you loathed so much."

"You just don't like him." Sal wrinkled her brow. Nothing helped, not talking, not the beer, nothing!

"I think the reason you're so miserable now is that you've known a breakup was inevitable." Abe made his point softly. "You've made very specific choices for your life. You gave up a thriving business, turned your back on a conventional nine-to-five existence. You know what you want, Sal, and for the life of me I don't see how Robert Capolla would fit in with any of your chosen plans."

Abe's words weighed on her. Her body felt hard and heavy and the thought of dragging herself out into the cool August air seemed next to impossible. She just wanted to sleep, to shut everything out and forget.

They drove back to the farm with all the windows rolled down, but still her head was reeling and the excruciating pain persisted. Abe was right, she thought. She had known from the start that there was no way her life could ever merge with Robert's. Not only that, it had been weeks since Robert had mentioned marriage.

Sal sighed. Oh, she had been such a fool to believe . . . well, she hadn't really believed he loved her or wanted to marry her. She had suspended her thinking, or thought she had. But somewhere, deep down, she knew she'd started to trust him, and though she hadn't really begun to nurture dreams of a future with him, she now realized those dreams had been there all along.

"I've been a fool." She hung her head out the window as Abe turned up the dusty lane.

"Someone's here, Sal!" Abe poked her between the shoulders.

Sal's eyes flew open at the sight of the strange car. She squinted, and as Abe's headlights flashed onto the license plate, Robert walked down the porch steps.

"Perfect timing." Abe gave a low whistle. "Maybe you should put off talking to him until tomorrow."

"Yes." Sal clenched her hands into damp fists. Dimly she knew she was in no condition to be rational, but the sight of him advancing toward her in his perfectly tailored, perfectly *perfect* suit infuriated her. Before she knew it she was out of Abe's car, striding toward him with fire in her eyes.

"Well, well . . ." Robert's expression was like a bucket of icy water. He walked past Sal and extended his hand to Abe. "I see we meet again."

"I was just dropping Sal off." Abe looked quickly at Sal, trying to sense what she expected his role to be in all of this. "We went out for a—"

"You don't have to explain!" Sal jumped in angrily. She whirled back to Robert. "I had no idea you were coming."

"Obviously." His accusatory eyes cut through her fury. She turned to Abe, signaling him to leave.

Abe hung back, reading the hostility in Robert. "She's had a lot to drink." He tried unsuccessfully to make eye contact with Robert. After several moments he turned and walked back to his car. "It's really very simple," he called out. "Sal needed to talk to somebody."

Robert did not reply. He waited until Abe's car was out of sight before speaking. "I must hand it to you. You trumped my trick again."

"I did nothing of the sort," Sal flared. "I told you I had no idea you'd show up."

"And the reason you didn't want me to come in the first place was so . . . basic." Robert gave her a snide smile.

"Not *basic* the way you mean." Sal marched up to the porch and sank down onto the steps with her hands on her knees. Suddenly she felt weak. A fight was the last thing she was ready for. "Basic," she went on after a moment, "if you mean I wanted time to myself, time for my work. Everything I said on the phone was true. I didn't have any prior plans with Abe."

"It's very difficult for me to believe anything you say." Robert seemed to tower over her, blocking off the slim crescent moon resting low on the horizon.

"That's your problem, isn't it?" Sal felt a renewed rush of fury. "I've never lied to you. If I had prior plans I would have told you. And don't . . ." She sprang to her feet and met his eyes. "Don't be so damned arrogant! You have no right to assume anything about me and what I do with my time when you're not here. I have a right to do anything I damn please, and so do you. I've always assumed that you have. Can you honestly tell me that you've never escorted a woman someplace since we've met? Can you swear you haven't bought another woman a drink or laughed or carried on a conversation?"

Robert faced her with a bullish, tight expression. He was hesitating too long.

"Of course you can't say that!" Sal jumped in triumphantly. "And I'd be a real fool if I expected that from you. I don't want to lock you in a cell, and I'll be damned if I'll be locked in one myself. You are not my keeper!"

She fled into the kitchen, slamming the door behind her. She stopped abruptly. Her mouth flew open and a faint cry escaped from her lips. The kitchen was filled with white roses.

CHAPTER SEVEN

"Roses," she sobbed. "Oh, no! Roses!" Stunned, with tears streaming down her cheeks, she moved slowly around the kitchen. They were everywhere—on the kitchen counter, the stove, the windowsills, in coffee cans on the floor, and of course, in the center of the old Formica table.

"Robert . . ." Sal collapsed into a chair and buried her head in her arms, crying softly.

He'd quietly entered the kitchen. "As soon as I hung up the phone I knew that conversation had been a stupid waste of time." He lifted her gently out of the chair and held her. "I figured it would be useless to call back. I knew I should wait until Friday, but I couldn't. I was on my way to the airport five minutes after I hung up."

He pressed his mouth against hers, breathing in her faint sobs and kissing her until she was filled with a new, rising urgency.

"I love you," she said. "Robert, I love you." The words tumbled out so easily, and now that they were

112

out her heart was pumping wildly and she was possessed with an even greater need for him.

Upstairs they undressed in the dark, feeling the silence in the old house as a protection. Sal felt his eyes on her as she stooped to pick up her slacks. He crossed over to her, catching her around the waist and turning her around until she felt seared against his warm flesh. She exhaled and the pain vanished as he moved in a slow hypnotic rhythm, inching her toward the bed.

Sal closed her eyes, wrapped her arms around his neck, and reveled in the delicious sensation of his tongue running along her neck, which arched backward over the bed. The soft hair on his muscular thighs triggered a deep sensual stirring, and when they both tumbled onto the bed she reached down to stroke his thighs.

They were beyond words now, beyond apologies and explanations, even beyond declarations of love and promises. Robert's hand moved with infinite care along the smooth tanned contour of her body. He rubbed back and forth, sensing each nuance as if he were memorizing her for all time. He paused at the generous curve of her hip, and as his mouth sought hers hungrily, he manipulated her onto her side so they were facing each other.

His tongue dipped deeper and she felt his desire, felt a new poignancy in his kisses, which sent hot waves surging through her. His hands spread tenderly over her breasts, cupping her, then pressing the flesh together, then gently kneading her. Her nipples, so sensitized by his tender petting, seemed to contract then expand until they were tingling.

"Yes . . ." Sal moaned and moved his head lower, so that his wet mouth took one pink nipple inside and sucked and flicked his tongue against its hard tip.

"Yes!" she cried again as he sucked harder. His

breathing accelerated and she felt his desire bursting and eager.

She covered him with her hand, stroking his firmness until he was quivering. His taut abdomen rose and fell rapidly, his mouth on her other nipple grew more profoundly insistent as she increased her pressure and guided him against her.

"Sal . . ." He breathed her name, a ragged plea as he tore his mouth from her breast and in one lightning-swift move rolled her over, filling her, loving her with that reckless rhythm she had grown to love.

The euphoric sensual fog enveloped her like hot steam. She wrapped her long legs around him, goading him on as she never had before. His hands dug into her back as he urged her to endure all of the wild pleasures he offered. It seemed they were rolling over and over, and each movement sent her soaring. She swiveled against him, felt him pause, and then, as if by mutual consent, they clutched desperately at each other before rocketing off into their own undulations of unparalleled sensual ecstasy.

"Are you glad I came down?" Robert cradled her in his arms and smoothed her damp forehead afterward.

"You know I am." Sal's eyelids fluttered. She was filled with peace, and her body seemed to be floating off in a celestial paradise. She turned and nuzzled against his shoulder. "Remind me to ask you tomorrow where you bought the roses." She smiled dreamily as she fell into a deep sleep.

The next morning she woke with a start to find the bed empty. She glanced at the clock. *Ten o'clock!* It had been months since she'd slept till ten o'clock! What about the chores?

The moment her feet hit the floor her anxiety burst into full bloom. She sat on the edge of the bed with a

114

stunned expression on her face as she recalled the details of the previous night. Today was Thursday, the day she had intended to make a new start for herself, the day she had intended to devote exclusively to her painting.

Well, at least she didn't have the chores to worry about, she thought. She'd arranged for the boys to take over her duties for the day. But where was Robert? And what was she going to do with him?

She hopped out of bed, feeling rattled. She ran her hands down her bare body and for an instant was immobilized by memories of last night's torrid lovemaking. But it was ten o'clock in the morning now and she could not, would not, allow those thoughts to dominate her.

She slipped into a T-shirt and her old overalls, went into the bathroom to brush her teeth and wash her face. She'd half expected to find Robert in there. In all the time she'd known him, he'd never once been up before her. To Sal, the lateness of the hour was symbolic of her lack of discipline. Ten o'clock was just too late!

Well, she decided, she would just tell him she couldn't go running off on one of his sightseeing trips, or spend hours over a leisurely lunch. She bounded into the kitchen, ready for the confrontation.

But he wasn't there. She glanced defensively at the roses and sniffed the air. Coffee. He must have put on the coffee. That was another thing he'd never done before.

She looked around warily as she poured a cup of steaming coffee. He'd left a box of her favorite doughnuts on the table. That meant he'd already driven into town. Puzzled, she sat down and dunked her doughnut in the hot liquid. Her eye traveled to a sheet of paper.

She picked it up gingerly and held her breath, expecting the worst.

> Dear Sal,
>   Eat all the doughnuts you want and have a good day painting. You won't have to put up with me till sundown. I'm making a reservation for dinner at the Boars Head Inn and you'd better be in a good mood.
> Love, Robert

Sal blinked, reread the note, started to laugh, and ended up crying. The relief flooded through her body. Three doughnuts later she was trudging through the woods with her painting paraphernalia. It was going to be a productive day. She just knew it was!

The next three weeks were almost too perfect to be believed. At first Sal had been sure that Robert's initial concession was simply a conciliatory gesture, but she was wrong. He seemed to have arrived at some unspoken new attitude regarding how she spent her time during his visits. Invariably he disappeared, if not the first thing in the morning, then shortly after she completed her farming chores. No matter how long or how short his visit was, he insisted she spend the afternoon on her work. The one exception was Sunday. Sunday, he maintained with his most charming smile, was the day he owned her. It was more than enough for Sal.

"Well, I'm insulted you've never introduced us." Sal's closest neighbors, Martha and Skip Gross, were sipping iced tea on Sal's back porch early one evening. Skip, a spry eighty year old with an impetuous child's curiosity and a bluntness to match, dropped the remark as Sal came out with a plate of cookies.

"It must be serious." Martha, slender as a reed and still beautiful at seventy-five, cast Sal a knowing smile.

"Oh, I don't know." Sal tried to shrug and Martha laughed.

"You're as bad a liar as Skip here," she said.

"No point in lying"—Skip helped himself to three cookies—"especially when you're my age."

"I bet you always spoke the truth." Sal perched herself on the porch railing and grinned at Skip. He really had a point. Next to Abe, Skip and Martha were her two closest friends, and yet she'd never arranged for them to meet Robert. It was as if everything concerning Robert was compartmentalized, as if they existed in a vacuum. He hadn't met her friends—unless you could count the two unfortunate encounters with Abe—and she hadn't met any of his. For the first time it struck her that there was something totally unrealistic about their exclusivity.

"Next time Robert comes down." She bobbed her head decisively. "Labor Day . . . this comin' weekend. I'm going to have a picnic. A cookout. Just the four of us, so you can really get acquainted."

"And also because you don't know anyone else." Skip chuckled as he popped another cookie in his mouth.

"It's his Yankee upbringing." Martha cast her husband a dry look which broke Sal up.

"Next Sunday night," she called after the elderly couple as they climbed into their car to leave.

After they drove off she flicked off the porch light, locked the door, and went upstairs to her studio to complete the painting she was working on. She stood inside her studio evaluating the work she'd done recently. She was improving, even Abe said so, and she knew she could rely on Abe to play it straight where her work was concerned. Since she'd really buckled down and began putting in more hours painting, she'd completed two paintings and was almost finished with a third.

Oddly enough, she always felt nervous the night before Robert was due to arrive, and he was supposed to fly down tomorrow, Friday. It was as if the intervening days reminded her that such perfection could not last. After all, she thought, how long would he be content to fly to Virginia every weekend? He'd already indicated that he was going to have to make a trip to California to see his children, and that the other children, the children who lived in London, would be coming to visit him for a month in December.

Sal dipped her brush into a dollop of burnt umber and forced her mind away from Robert and what might or might not happen. For the next two hours she was immersed in her work. Only when she crawled into bed around ten thirty did a sharp fear sweep over her. Robert hadn't called as he usually did the night before he flew down.

The next morning she was listless and enervated, snapping at Abe and irritable with her mother on the phone. She kept the cordless phone with her even when she went down to the vegetable stand at the foot of the lane. There was no way she could have missed his call. Back at the house she forced herself to pack up her painting gear. The remote phone was not effective way out in the woods, but she would just have to risk missing a call. As she was about to leave, the phone finally rang.

"Yes?" She answered breathlessly, praying it was Robert saying he was already at the airport.

"This is Mr. Capolla's secretary." The voice at the other end of the line was chilly. "He's asked me to let you know that he won't be arriving as planned this weekend."

Sal's stomach tightened as the secretary went on to explain that some business contingency precluded Robert's arrival in Charlottesville, but that he would phone her as soon as possible.

The kiss of doom? Sal wondered, staring at the phone after she hung up. Maybe he had been seeing someone else in New York. If so, she thought, it was her own fault. She stormed out of the kitchen and stood in the yard under the glaring sun. The late summer sun . . . yes, it seemed to her the air had a different feel to it now, more stifling, less promising. Everything in her garden was wilting, the grass dried and brown.

She knew she could have gone to New York, could have suggested it at least once. But no, she berated herself—she had been so rigid. In a way, she was as rigid as Robert when it came to certain attitudes. But Robert had altered his rigidity, she thought: After that one horrible episode he had simply changed. He had given her the time she needed. And what had she given him?

Sal paced around the perimeter of the yard, chastising herself. She had no doubt that he would call, and assumed she would probably see him again. Only she wondered whether it wouldn't be different. Maybe he had already begun to tire of their arrangement. Maybe he had found someone who suited him better.

Sal leaned against the fence post and stared at the herd of cattle as they swatted their tails in each other's faces to keep the flies away. The farm was finally coming together for her. The herd had almost doubled and by next spring she would begin realizing some profits on her investment. She had made excellent choices, buying top quality livestock. She could already see that her idea of balancing a life as a painter with the running of a farm was a valid one. And she loved it. No, she told herself—she couldn't give this up.

119

She turned around and looked back up toward the old house. Robert had wanted to have it painted, but lately he hadn't mentioned it. Just like he never mentioned marriage anymore. And when was the last time he'd said he loved her? she wondered. Maybe they were all just words.

Yes, Robert was a man for the moment, Sal thought —impetuous, dramatic, full of a lust for life, devouring. Maybe he had thought better of marriage. Maybe that was why he hadn't brought the subject up again. Maybe he had finally concluded that a man who had already failed twice should give a third marriage more than cursory consideration. But then, she mused, maybe he had decided that twice was enough, that she was the wrong woman for him.

This led Sal to realize that over the course of the summer she had lost sight of what a high risk candidate he really was; a man with two ex-wives and four children. She knew a number of divorced people. Anyone could make one mistake. But two?

By nightfall, Sal was in the throes of depression. She was back to square one. Robert was not the sort of man she needed in her life, she'd decided, but she loved him. She sat on the side porch, rocking furiously. The crickets singing in the bushes made her yearn for him, every lingering summer sound like a passionate signal. She loved him, and his absence transformed the lovely night litany into a fugue.

By Sunday she was numb to the stinging pain which had been her initial reaction. She forced herself to be objective in the face of her disappointment. Whatever happened, she would continue with her life as planned. The summer had lulled her into complacency in more ways than one. She couldn't expect to live on Robert's farm forever, she told herself. In fact, living here only complicated a situation that was already complicated enough. Initially, she had been uneasy about Robert being her landlord. Then it had become a joke between them. Finally, she had taken it all for granted; almost forgotten. Now she was once again uneasy. Only this time, she decided, she was going to do something about it.

Instead of going to the local real estate agent, Harry O'Brien, she contacted a large firm in Charlottesville. Harry would tell Robert, and maybe Robert would think it was some sort of ploy on her part when all she wanted was to find property and a house she could afford to buy. Her life was here in the Shenandoah, and she was going to prove it.

"I think I've found a house." She phoned Skip and Martha late Monday evening and asked them to accompany her to the new property late Tuesday afternoon. Now that she had decided to go for broke, she was anxious to have everything settled. While this piece of land was nowhere near as spectacular as Robert's property, it did have some valuable attributes. It was a working farm, and the barn and two other outbuildings were in reasonably good shape. There were only ten acres, but there was an option on another fifty located across the road. The house was a mess, but then, she was used to primitive living conditions.

"It's a good buy!" Skip observed when they came back and were having a beer on Sal's porch.

"It's a lot of money," Sal mused. Her heart was pounding. It was an enormous commitment. The mortgage would be breathtaking, but it was the idea of the commitment, of putting herself on the line, that intrigued her. If need be, she thought, she could always take on a couple of accounts, free lance, with her old office. One dynamite campaign would help offset her expenses.

"I think I'm going to do it!" She jumped up from her rocking chair just as a car drove up the driveway.

"Company." Skip looked amused at the flabbergasted expression on Sal's face as a silver Mercedes stopped and Robert Capolla jumped out and sprinted up to the porch.

"Robert . . . ?" Sal gaped at him. He was wearing jeans and a T-shirt that said Save the Whales. Even on Sundays she'd never seen him so casually attired.

She stammered through introductions, aware that Skip was getting an enormous kick out of her flustered behavior.

"I'll get you a beer." She escaped inside and pressed her head against the refrigerator for relief as the screen door slammed and Robert walked in, closing the wooden back door behind him.

"You drove all the way?" She faced him with a bewildered expression.

He kissed her on the tip of the nose and brushed a lock of hair out of her face. "I tried calling you last night, then again this morning from New York, and again from Washington this afternoon."

"You caught me off guard." Sal handed him a can of beer. She backed away from him as if she could ward off the impact of his unexpected appearance.

"Jenny called and explained what happened, didn't she?" He looked concerned.

"If Jenny is your secretary." Sal glanced toward the back door, half expecting to see Skip with his ear pressed to the keyhole.

"Yes, Jenny is my secretary. She called and explained why I couldn't make it for the weekend, didn't she?"

"She said some business came up," Sal said tightly.

122

"You're kidding. That's all she said?" He slammed the can of beer down on the table, spilling the foam.

Sal leaped to wipe up the foam, as if she had suddenly turned into the most domestic of creatures and this was her best antique table instead of a Formica relic.

"She didn't tell you there was a problem with my daughter and that she and her mother flew over from London so we could try to straighten matters out?"

Sal shook her head. A flicker of excitement fluttered in her breast as she sopped up the spilled beer.

"Maybe it's my fault!" he stormed. "I should have told her to deliver a personal message. Business? She just said I had business?"

"It's all right. . . ." Sal touched his arm tentatively.

"You're upset." He placed his hands on her shoulders and looked at her steadily. "No wonder." He drew her close and pressed his lips against the top of her head. "It's my fault, not Jenny's. I should have been more explicit."

"It's all right." Sal's eyes were glistening as she gazed into his dark, luminous eyes. "But why did you drive down?"

A sly smile played on his lips. "I brought my papers . . . my files, my itty-bitty night-light, and my three favorite records. I've arranged to carry on business down here. I'm moving in."

CHAPTER EIGHT

"Moving in?" Sal asked incredulously. "What do you mean moving in?" She stared at him, aghast, heart pounding, pulse racing. She had thought it was all over, and now this. She was shocked, but also flattered, confused, excited, and terrified.

"How can you be moving in? I wasn't sure I'd ever hear from you again—"

Robert silenced her with a deep, yearning kiss which took her breath away and for the moment stopped her from thinking. "We'll discuss it later." He gazed at her lovingly. "You have company. Or did you forget?"

"I didn't forget." Sal gaped at him. "I can't remember . . . did I introduce you?"

"You were your usual charming self." Robert picked up his beer and went outside to join Skip and Martha.

Sal stood rooted to the kitchen floor with the same dumbfounded expression on her face. Phrases like "how dare he" and "who does he think he is" bounced ambivalently around inside her mind. She wondered if she shouldn't be angry at his audacious assumption, especially after the miserable weekend she'd gone through. But she wasn't angry, just relieved. In fact, she was all goosebumpy and shivery. She wished Skip and Martha would beat a quick retreat, but when she went back out to the porch, she found them chatting easily with Robert. While she listened, he had invited the elderly couple to join them for a lobster dinner.

"You drove all the way from New York with four live lobsters?" Sal's voice rang with unprecedented excitement.

"Six," Robert corrected her as he trotted out to his car.

Martha caught Sal's eye and winked, signaling her approval. Skip was unusually taciturn, but over the next hour, while they put together a salad to go with the lobster, Sal saw that he was being totally won over by Robert. By the end of the evening they were all laughing and gabbing away as if they'd been friends forever.

As Robert walked the elderly couple to their car, Sal stood in the shadows on the back porch and listened to their laughter with a curious half smile. The evening was a complete revelation to her. She had never imagined that Robert would fit in, that he would appreciate Skip's wry humor or Martha's genteel, keen intellect. She had imagined that an evening spent with the Grosses would be too dull for Robert. Now she saw how badly she had underestimated him.

The low hum of voices lulled her. Robert was relating an anecdote about all the stumbling blocks the automobile industry was throwing in his way. She liked the way he talked about his work, liked that he wanted to share his recent frustrations not just with her but with Skip and Martha as well. And there was nothing preachy or arrogant in his conversation, nothing in his manner that set him apart as the dashing, brilliant young millionaire who had appeared on the cover of *Time* magazine.

Maybe he had changed, Sal thought. She folded her arms and leaned against the screen door, half listening to Robert's story. She recalled him as he had been that first day, standing so stiffly, so arrogantly. Then he had been an image, tonight he was himself—a man, warm and generous, easy, relaxed.

"I like your friends," he told her as they watched them drive away. He tasted her lips hungrily and wrapped his arm around her waist as they went inside.

"Robert . . ."

He covered her mouth in a deep, penetrating kiss. His tongue slid slowly in and out, tantalizing her, promising her.

"No thinking tonight." His dark eyes burned into her. "No talking . . ." He ran his hands over her breasts, arousing her so quickly, so fully, that she gasped.

"Oh, I've missed you, Sal." His fingers were like fire ripping at her blouse. She didn't care. She arched toward him, and as he unfastened her bra she took off her blouse.

"You're not expecting anyone, are you?" he whispered as he nipped impatiently at her full breasts.

"No . . ." she moaned as he titillated her nipple. She was bursting with desire. Great torrents of liquid fire seemed to gush from her. She could think only of his powerful thrusts and how it felt to hold him in her arms.

He had removed his shirt and she ran her hands along his well-defined muscular chest, testing the wiry hairs, relishing each detail of his virility as if for the first time. How she had missed him!

And how he had missed her! She felt his urgency as

never before, felt him against her as she fumbled with his belt.

"There's something about this kitchen, Sal," he murmured as he helped her out of her slacks and bent to slide her panties down her long, tanned legs.

"This kitchen is a virtual den of erotic iniquity." He showered kisses up her leg, pausing to run his tongue along the inside of her thigh. "You're so beautiful." She felt his dark hair pressing against her thighs, and the agony of her desire was so excruciatingly sweet that she cried out.

His hands caressed her as he knelt in front of her, nuzzling into her, drinking in all the moist sweetness.

"There's no one like you." He staggered to his feet and stared into her eyes. His eyes were black coals, bright with that reckless desire which only he possessed. Sal's nipples swelled as he pressed her against his chest.

"I dreamed of you . . . of this moment." Robert stroked her until she was hot and on the verge of erupting. He was primed, they both were, and yet they were suspended, both luxuriating in the matchless eroticism of the moment.

Slowly, Robert guided her to him in an erotic dance. She clung to him, panting softly as he moved against her in a fascinating sensual rhythm. She wrapped her arms around his neck as he lifted her off the floor. She had no idea what he was doing—there were only sensations, torrents of wild, hot, flowing sensations.

Instinctively she wrapped her legs around his waist, groaning with pleasure as her body came into even closer contact with him. She wriggled against him as if she could enter his powerful virile body.

"I want to give you every pleasure," he said hoarsely. "It's been over a week, Sal. I'm going to prove how much I missed you!"

Beads of perspiration broke out along her spine as he unwound her legs from around his waist and slid her damp body against his. His control was masterly. They were both trembling with desire.

"I wanted to make love to you here that first day." He eased her back onto the table, gently. "Yes . . ." With his eyes on hers, he slid into her. Lifting her up and holding her firmly, began to move in the same erotic, dancelike movement.

Sal gasped, exploding, convulsing, crying out. She was hurled into a sensual oblivion unlike anything she had ever known. Nothing else existed, only Robert and his power, his rhythm. He throbbed into her harder and harder, taking risks, pausing then plunging ahead to a cataclysmic climax.

They clung to each other, still trembling, still overcome by convulsive aftershocks. His heart thundered against her and she placed her hand over it.

"Robert, I'm a big woman . . . you might want to put me down now, honey."

Robert gave her a dazed smile as they parted. He kissed her tenderly and they stared at each other, their naked bodies gleaming white in the moonlight flooding into the kitchen.

"I think I've outdone myself. . . ." He collapsed into a chair and hung his head between his legs.

"How about some saltines?" Sal bent down and kissed the nape of his neck.

The next morning she awoke to find Robert fast asleep next to her. She flushed, recalling last night's scene in the kitchen. Afterward they had devoured a box of saltines and a quart of milk. After Robert's dazzling performance, she thought, it was likely he'd sleep all day.

Sal stifled a giggle as she glanced at his face. Of

course, there had been nothing amusing in their torrid lovemaking last night. Only today, she felt all giggly remembering. Well, leave it to Robert to come up with a novel approach, she thought—she would never have to worry about becoming bored with him around.

She frowned suddenly, remembering the announcement preceding their lovemaking. Was she really ready to have Robert around all the time? Was she ready to live with him? She slipped out of bed, went into the bathroom, and stood under an icy shower.

Live with Robert Capolla? She knew exactly what it would mean. It would mean a phone with five buttons, or even two phones with five buttons. It would mean more obligations, and fighting for every minute she spent in her studio, painting.

In terms of being sensitive to her needs as an artist, she thought, he had improved enormously. Only she was so conscious of it all, so anxious to be fair about the way she spent her time. Even that took energy.

For an instant she felt jittery, worried she would never achieve anything with her art, that she was really just a dilettante, a dabbler. She chastised herself that since she'd met Robert she hadn't been working at it seriously enough: She really should have much more to show for herself by now, shouldn't she?

Downstairs, Sal put on the coffee before going out to give Wendell special instructions for the day. The boys would be returning to school next week and she would have to find someone else to assist her with the morning chores. Abe was low on money and she'd considered asking him to help, but she decided that with Robert around that might not be a tactful idea. Robert had made no real effort to get to know Abe, still resenting the close bond—both professional and personal—Sal had with Abe.

"Wendell!" She waved to him, and after a brief chat returned to the kitchen for a cup of coffee. There was a bit of chill in the air and the coffee warmed her and made her almost eager for winter.

How was Robert going to carry on his business from Blue Mills, Virginia? Why had he chosen this particular moment to make his move? After the second cup of coffee Sal's mind began zipping along toward a logical conclusion. By the third cup her mind felt clear. She was definitely *not* ready to cohabit with Robert Capolla, even if it was his house.

She went back outside, finished her chores, and when she returned around eleven, Robert was dressed in jeans and a T-shirt, sipping his coffee.

"Is this the new you?" Sal kissed him on the cheek and sat down across from him.

"Maybe so." He grinned. "Don't I deserve a day off, oh wielder of the Puritan Ethic?"

Sal laughed. "You drove ten hours yesterday, not to mention what you did once you arrived. All right, you can have the day off."

"Thank you." Robert gave her a sly smile.

Sal twisted her hands nervously, then jumped right into the dreaded subject. "Robert, I don't know what prompted you but I . . . I don't think it'd be a good idea for you to move in."

Robert's head jerked to attention, and for a moment Sal regretted her decision.

"It doesn't feel right to me, Robert. It feels . . . sort of patchwork." She met his eyes squarely, and for the first time it dawned on her why it felt so patchwork. For the first time she wondered why he had suggested cohabitation instead of marriage. Something in her began to recoil. Without wanting to, without really meaning to, she felt suspicious.

"You didn't give it much thought." Robert looked chagrined.

"Yes, I did. I thought about it all morning. As a matter of fact, I've decided to buy another house. You can stay here and—"

"No, no," Robert interrupted quickly. "I'm the landlord but you have your rights here. You have a lease until January."

"And then you'll ask me to leave?" Sal tensed.

"I'm trying to understand, Sal." Robert got up and poured himself another cup of coffee. "Don't get your back up. I'm the one who's been turned down here. And maybe you're right. Maybe it would be better if we had separate places. At least I'll be down here most of the time, instead of commuting to New York."

"What about your office? What about the car?"

"A lot of problems." Robert grimaced, and for the first time she was aware that he seemed thinner, that there was a haggard, worn look around his eyes. Last night he had been so relaxed, so ebullient, she hadn't noticed.

"I'm sorry, Robert." So there were problems and he had retreated. To lick his wounds? she wondered. Was that why he'd decided to relocate for the time being?

"The last tests on the battery were far from satisfactory. Several investors are getting nervous. I'm not exactly the man of the hour right now. I thought some time away might give me a better perspective. And"— he smiled sadly—"I rather like it down here, in case you haven't noticed."

"I'm sorry about the tests." Sal reached for his hand.

"I like a challenge," he said. "Obstacles don't really bother me. I'll figure it out eventually."

"I'm the same way." Sal met his eyes in unspoken acknowledgment of some deeper struggle going on both

131

between them, and in each separately. "I'll figure things out too."

"And now"—he stood up abruptly—"I am off to find some suitable habitat for myself. I'm thinking something near a running stream. I've never fished. Think I'd like to try . . . but purely for academic reasons. Don't expect fish for dinner, Sal. I intend to throw them all back."

On that rather enigmatic remark he left her staring after him. After a while, Sal smiled. He had taken her ultimatum better than she had anticipated. Time was what was needed, she thought, and time was what they finally had. Time together. Maybe there was a chance after all.

The next week was by far the most productive she had spent since moving back to Virginia. With Robert ensconced in his somewhat dismal little shack overlooking Blue Mills Falls, they fell into a steady, reliable, if offbeat routine. Sal rose as usual at five, did her chores, and joined Robert for breakfast at nine. Then they both went their separate ways—Robert to fish and read, or, as she supposed, to make occasional phone calls and write letters related to his business; and Sal to paint, either down by the stream or in her studio. Evenings they ate out, either traveling to one of the surrounding inns or hitting the local hamburger joints. Then they went home—hers or his, depending on how they looked at it—to make love. It shocked Sal that there were no problems. Not one. Robert kept a book and his itty-bitty light next to *his* side of *her* bed, and after they made love he would read while she went to sleep. It was all astonishingly easy.

On Tuesday of Robert's second week as a full-time resident of Albemarle County, Sal put the finishing touches on a small but particularly successful painting.

In the mood to celebrate, she decided to pop in unexpectedly on Robert.

She rolled the windows of her old station wagon down as she drove along the rutted dirt road which led to his log cabin. The maples were already stained a fiery red, and the nip of fall was in the air. She leaned out the window, craned her neck, and slowed down to watch a hawk circling in the bright-blue September sky. She had never in her life baked an apple pie, but suddenly she was overcome by a fervent desire to do so. She smiled as she drove on. Robert would get a good laugh out of that.

She parked her car next to his and stood a moment with her hands in her jeans pockets, appreciating the solitude of his woodsy retreat. Dilapidated and primitive as it was, it oddly enough seemed to suit his needs for the moment.

She knocked several times and when no one answered crept inside, calling softly in case he had fallen asleep while reading. But the narrow daybed was empty and a quick look around the tiny dwelling confirmed that he was not there. He was probably fishing, she thought. As Sal headed for the door her eye fell on a picture on the front page of *The New York Times.* It was a photograph of Robert.

She grabbed the paper and scanned the article with a sense of disbelief. She sank into a chair, read the article again, and then turned back to the front page to check the date. The paper was three days old. Robert hadn't mentioned a word. Recent testing on his battery-run automobile had revealed grave flaws in the concept and the company was being forced to declare bankruptcy. And he hadn't mentioned a word about it!

"Robert!" Sal shot out of the cabin and ran down toward the rocky streambed. Why had he kept it to himself? she wondered. Didn't he trust her? Or was he so upset that he couldn't even find the words?

Suddenly Sal panicked. For all of his arrogance and sophisticated charm she knew now that at heart Robert Capolla was a romantic, a visionary whose intellect would always be devoted to some future ideal. His obsession with his new automobile went far beyond that of pure economics. It even went beyond his ego, which was undeniably overwhelming. Robert believed in that car as he believed in a future that would somehow be more perfect than the past. He had been ridiculed for his notions. But then, he joked that all great men were ridiculed for their innovative ideas.

"Robert!" She called his name repeatedly, running along the narrow streambed until she came to the falls. He wasn't there, she realized. He simply wasn't there!

She ran back to the cabin, telling herself that she was overreacting. Robert was not the sort of person to do something irrational. Back inside his cabin she reread the piece in the *Times*. The implication was that Robert had taken advantage of his investors, had allowed his ego to outweigh his sense of business ethics.

The implication angered Sal. She knew it simply wasn't true. Robert genuinely believed in his concept. He had discussed it with her. He had employed the best scientific minds on its behalf and he had listened to them. On paper his concept was flawless. A battery-run automobile would be a godsend. Not only would it eliminate the reliance on fossil fuels, it would contribute considerably to a cleaner environment and would ultimately be cost-efficient.

But she knew it was still thought to be a crackpot notion, and many people in high places were threatened by what such an enormous shift in technology would

134

portend. Sal hurled the *Times* across the cabin and stomped back outside, calling him.

"I'm here. . . ." She wheeled around at the sound of his voice. He moseyed toward her as if nothing unusual had happened. If he hadn't been dressed in a somber blue business suit, she might have thought she imagined the whole thing.

"Why didn't you tell me?" Sal ran to him and threw her arms around his neck.

"I don't know." He looked back along the path that led into the woods, as if his thoughts were still there beneath the flaming trees.

"Did you know when you came down here? Robert, was it really business after all, and not your . . . daughter that kept you away that weekend?" There was a new urgency in Sal's voice. Things were bad enough, but suddenly they were worse, more complicated. Suddenly she felt used. Robert had fled to Blue Mills not because of her but because he'd needed to escape.

"It's not what you're thinking, Sal," he said wearily.

"Why is it you think you can always read my mind!" she flared. "Robert, you drove down here without warning and announced you wanted us to live together and—"

"Please!" He grabbed her arm, silencing her with the pressure of his fingers. His face was contorted in a painful grimace. She had the distinct feeling that one more word from her might cause him to collapse in tears, or explode in anger. The enormous pressure he had been under had taken its toll.

"Yes, I did lie," he said, releasing her arm with an apologetic glance. "My daughter had nothing to do with it. That night, when I had my secretary call to say I wouldn't be down, I should have told her to be more explicit with you. You're right about that. She had or-

135

ders not to tell anyone what was happening. But I guess I assumed she would be more tactful where you were concerned."

Sal was beset with a barage of conflicting emotions. She felt sorry for him, for all the problems he was having, but she also resented his silence, his lying, and all of the additional complications he had foisted on their relationship.

"Sal, I was rattled when I gave Jenny orders to call you and say I wouldn't be here. Things were happening awfully fast. It felt like my world was caving in. All my plans, everything was disintegrating. Don't you see? I wasn't thinking. And then when I got down here I could see you were still angry, that the explanation had not been enough for you. I could see plainly that you didn't want to think that business could ever come between us, so I made up a story I thought you would find more acceptable, something more personal, more emotional. Look, Skip and Martha were outside waiting. It didn't seem like a good time to get into long explanations!"

He took her by the shoulders and looked beseechingly into her eyes. "Sal, I was so glad to see you. I didn't want to fight, didn't want to think anymore. I saw how upset you were and it seemed like you'd prefer a different story, so I gave you one."

"That easily?" Sal was stung. He had lied. Maybe she didn't know him very well after all, she thought.

"It made you feel better, didn't it?" Robert massaged her shoulders lightly, but she pulled away.

She shook her head. "At the moment, yes. But it was a lie. When you told me your daughter was having problems, it was all a lie?"

"Not all." Robert narrowed his dark eyes. He seemed

136

detached, isolated. "She had problems in the past. I said it had just happened. A trick of time."

Sal bit back a caustic comment. This was hardly the time to start an argument, she thought, or to throw up his faulty sense of morality to him.

"Sal, I didn't think I'd have to explain to you what this means to me. My whole life has been wrapped up in this car battery for the past seven years. No, more really. All my life I've nurtured this idea. Oh, I won't say everything I've done has been geared to seeing its fruition, but—"

"Robert, I understand that!" Sal burst out. "I know how much it means to you. But how could you have kept it to yourself?"

"I don't know." He looked completely deflated. "But I didn't come to Blue Mills just to lick my wounds. You can't believe that."

"I don't know what I believe." Sal turned away from him.

"I'd been thinking about spending a few months down here even before everything started to fall apart with the car."

Sal turned back and met his eyes for a moment. "You're going someplace?" She indicated his crisply tailored suit. It was the first time she'd seen him in a suit since his relocation.

"New York. If I don't give a press conference soon, they'll be accusing me of being a spy, or a thief."

"Were you going to tell me?" Sal stepped in front of him and forced him to look at her.

"I was." He met her eyes after a moment. "I was going to stop off on my way to the airport. I just went for a walk . . . to clear my mind for the zillionth time. Sal, I can see what you're thinking. You think I'm terrible—like all the rest."

"I don't!" Sal denied it vehemently, though moments before she had been thinking exactly that.

"I lied to you," he said.

"Maybe you had a reason." Sal looked at him closely, then turned away abruptly, the tears stinging in her eyes. Did he really love her? she wondered. Or was she just a convenience? Good ol' Sal . . . someone awfully nice, who didn't make too many demands.

"Does it bother you that I'm bankrupt?" he asked after a moment.

"Of course it doesn't!" Sal exclaimed.

Robert smiled ruefully. "It's a technicality, of course. I'm still rich by any reasonable standards. One company goes bankrupt, but I still have my own money and other businesses. The law allows people like me some cushions."

"I understand about all that." Sal followed him to his Mercedes. "I don't give a damn about your money, Robert. I never did. I love you. . . ."

She took his face between her two hands and gave him a long, searching look. "Please come back soon, Robert. I need you."

CHAPTER NINE

And she did need him, more than she had ever realized, more than she had ever thought possible. She missed him more, much more than she would have liked. By the last week in September her nerves were on edge from too many unsatisfactory long distance phone calls. Of course, she understood that his life was being made miserable by the press, that he was drained and exhausted from the negative publicity. She knew he was working day and night trying to salvage as many business relationships as possible. His credibility was low. He needed to speak directly to people in order to reestablish the bond of trust. She knew he needed to do this for himself, not just for future business ventures. It was a question of honor, despite what they were saying about him in the newspapers.

But it was hard. Suddenly her life in Blue Mills seemed remote, almost vacuous. Skip and Martha both thought she should go to New York. But the one time she had suggested it, Robert's response had been cool.

That, of course, had only increased her anxiety. Maybe on top of everything else, she thought, he was letting go of her as well.

Finally, unable to endure the ambiguities or her imagination a moment longer, she impulsively drove to the Charlottesville airport and boarded Piedmont's final flight to New York. It was Friday night and the plane was brimming with businessmen. For a moment she felt stifled in the not-so-distant past, when her life had revolved around men such as these.

She ordered a Scotch and drank it quickly, trying to dispel her nervousness. She was not an impulsive person. She had almost phoned him at the last minute, but afraid that his response would dampen her resolve, she had decided against it. She stared at the pointy toes of her brown high heels. She was wearing one of her old work uniforms, as she called it—a chic, well-cut, brown tweed jacket with a brown velvet collar, a matching pencil-slim skirt, and a white silk blouse. Her sun-streaked hair was wound into a tight, neat chignon, and she was wearing tiny gold-drop earrings Robert had given her. She was totally unaware of the admiring glances of her male traveling companions.

It was probably a dumb move, she thought, as she taxied from La Guardia Airport into Manhattan. At least she should have phoned him from the airport. But it was too late for that. She paid the cab driver and turned toward Robert's Park Avenue apartment building, an old monolithic pre-World War II edifice. Just as the doorman reached for the door, she turned back to the street, her heart pounding.

What on earth was she thinking of coming up here unannounced? she asked herself. Hadn't she criticized him for just such presumptuous behavior? She shifted her small valise from one hand to the other as she stood

140

on the curb. If Robert had wanted her here, she thought, wanted her support, he would have asked.

She frowned. How unfortunate, not to mention costly, that it had taken a trip to New York to enable her to see things clearly. She told herself that the truth was, he didn't need her. The truth was, his temporary relocation had had far more to do with the stressful situation created by the bankruptcy than it did with her.

Sal walked aimlessly down Park Avenue toward the midtown Manhattan halo of lights. A hollow ache was forming in her chest, making it difficult to breathe. How stupid she had been to think that he was moving to Blue Mills because of her, she thought—so that they could share their days without his having to hop on a plane every Monday. She had seen the move as a prelude to something more permanent. But like everything else in Robert Capolla's life, it had been business related, a calculated interval affording him the opportunity to rally and partially recover before returning to the front. And now he was back in the line of fire, back where he wanted to be.

Sal stopped walking and frowned. Wasn't she being just a bit hard on him? It was his business after all, his baby, so to speak. Of course, he would do everything he could to rescue the project. There was nothing unusual in that, she thought. Maybe what was stinging her was that his response was so typical. He had neither confided the impending disaster to her nor sought her intellect or her solace in the wake of all the negative publicity. He was a lone operator. Like too many men she had known, he compartmentalized his life.

She shivered as she rounded the corner at Fifty-seventh Street. It was much colder up here than it had been in Virginia. She paused to look at the expensive crystal in the Baccarat display window, thinking how odd that she had finally come to New York and was wandering around the city by herself. Maybe there was some value in that, she mused, though it was hardly romantic.

Farther west on Fifty-seventh Street she paused at one of the city's most reputable art galleries, and for a while, as she lost herself in the paintings, thoughts of Robert receded. So this was the New York art scene, she thought. In the back of her mind it had seemed formidable, beyond her. But now, seeing the work of a highly touted artist, she felt heartened. By comparison, her recent paintings had a clarity of vision, an originality altogether absent from these paintings. Something in her quickened, and the surge of confidence spilled over onto thoughts of Robert.

She headed for the nearest phone booth, wedged herself and her valise inside, and dug in her purse for a quarter. She'd decided not to take Robert's silence personally, that it would be self-indulgent and petty to do so. After all, she had known all along that he was an obsessed businessman. No one made five million dollars before he was forty without being obsessed!

"Robert, it's me!" Sal grimaced at the sound of his answering machine.

"Robert, it's Sal," she repeated when the electronic beep signaled that it was time for her to leave a message. "I've done something pretty impulsive—I've come to New York. I have to talk to you. I hope you didn't fly to Virginia."

She took a deep breath and rushed on before the tape could run out. "I'm heading for the Waldorf. Call me there, unless you're in London, Paris . . . or Blue Mills."

An hour later Sal lay soaking in a tub in a modest room at the Waldorf-Astoria. Of course, there were cheaper hotels in New York. Only it seemed that once she had blundered into such an extravagant impulsive course, it was foolish not to go all the way. The only thing that would rescue her from feeling absolutely ridiculous was a sense of humor.

She sank into the tub and reached for the martini room service had delivered at her request. It never even occurred to her to have a martini in Blue Mills, but once her heels hit the city pavement the thought of that dry icy liquid crossed her mind every time. She smiled, feeling tipsy and strangely calm after so many conflicting emotions.

Maybe she'd needed to get away from Blue Mills, she thought, and Robert. Oh, yes, Robert was Blue Mills. Since July the place had been totally altered by his presence. She could not look at the blue Shenandoahs without thinking of him. But summer was over now.

Sal sipped her martini pensively, thinking of the rolling hills, the hearty fecundity of the Virginia air. She had conveniently managed to forget about when and if she might put a binder on the piece of property she had been considering before Robert moved down. Now she knew, beyond a shadow of a doubt, that she needed a place all her own. Lying in scented luxury in one of New York's ritziest hotels, she knew for certain where her true home was.

Sal toweled herself dry and tried to steer her thoughts away from Robert. She'd picked up a current best-selling mystery in the hotel store and snuggled into bed with the book. In lieu of Robert, she thought, smiling at the irony: It had been months since she'd gone to bed with a book.

The next morning she woke at her usual hour, phoned room service again, and indulged in a leisurely breakfast in bed. By ten o'clock she was antsy. Why hadn't he called? she wondered. She phoned the desk to make certain there wasn't a message, but no one had called.

She'd circled several interesting art shows in *The New York Times,* thinking she would talk Robert into playing hookey and they'd spend a few hours together. She stared listlessly at the paper, debating whether she shouldn't just fly straight back to Virginia.

But that was stupid, she decided: to fly all the way to New York on impulse, and just because she couldn't make an immediate connection with him, fly back home. She dialed his apartment again and was heartened when she received a busy signal. She dressed rapidly, trying the number again every few minutes. The next time she tried, the line was clear, and her heart accelerated with each ring. It was going to be all right. She would see Robert in his city, on his turf. They would go to galleries, have lunch at one of his favorite spots. It was something she should have done a long time ago. She wanted to see his office, suddenly wanted to know what kind of rug he walked on, what color sheets he slept on. . . .

"You've reached 351. . . ." The answering machine message had clicked on and she listened to Robert's voice.

"Damn!" She slammed the receiver down. She'd missed him! Or maybe the line had been tied up with another call and he'd never even been there. Either way, she felt like crying.

Well, maybe he was at his office, she thought. She dialed the number and girded herself for his secretary's cool, protective response. "Jenny, this is Sal Carter. Is Robert there by any chance?"

"I'll give him a message," came the guarded reply.

"I'm up here," Sal rushed on. "I'm in New York—"

"He's asked me to hold all calls."

"Then he's there . . . ?" Sal was suddenly desperate to hear his voice. It occurred to her that something else had gone wrong, that his affairs had taken another turn for the worse.

"I'm sorry, Sal." There was a note of softness in Jenny's voice. "I really can't disturb him."

"Is he all right?" She fought back her tears, fought back the urge to demand, to slam down the receiver and walk straight over to his Madison Avenue office and see for herself.

"Can he reach you somewhere?" Jenny had never been this warm before. Why? Did that mean Robert was in greater trouble, or that Jenny felt sorry for her because—

"The Waldorf. I . . . I'll be going out, but I'll check back from time to time. I'm free for lunch if he is. I'll be flying back to Virginia on the seven-thirty flight."

The day was brilliant, sunny and perfect. The city buzzed with a friendly liveliness, and the three art shows she went to were stimulating—innovative and at the same time encouraging. Everything about the day reminded her of how much more it would have meant had Robert been with her. But there were no messages. By late afternoon, as she sat sipping a cup of coffee in the little dining room adjacent to the sculpture garden at the Whitney Museum, she was drained of all hope. She was absolutely certain that Robert Capolla had disappeared from her life.

His silence could only mean that, she'd decided—unless Jenny didn't know where he was.

Sal could not stop trying to puzzle it out. Upstairs at the Whitney she stood staring at Calder's whimsical circus trying to dispel the heaviness which had overtaken her. She should have come to New York sooner, she thought, and that was gnawing at her. She had waited too long.

She walked back to her hotel. She had checked out earlier but had left her valise at the desk.

"You have a call, Miss Carter."

She practically jumped over the reservations counter in response.

"There's a courtesy phone just over there." The clerk gestured off to the right.

"I just got your message." Robert sounded perfectly dreadful, his voice hoarse and faint with exhaustion.

"Is everything all right?" Sal wanted to weep with relief.

"No, of course not." He gave a callous laugh.

"I miss you," Sal said instinctively. "That's why I flew up without calling. I miss you, Robert. I just wanted to see you . . . if only for a—"

"It's a bad time," he interrupted wearily.

"I know it is." Sal brushed a lock of hair out of her face and reminded herself to be patient, not to be upset by his preoccupied tone.

"Look, Robert, I don't want to be another complication in your life. I know how hard you must be working. I just thought a few hours together might lighten your load. I'm scheduled for the seven thirty out of La Guardia, but I suppose I could cancel—"

"Sal," he interrupted, "the thing is, you've picked a terrible time."

"I think you've made that clear." Sal flushed. She felt like an intruder, like just another business colleague who was making demands on him.

"I probably shouldn't have called," he said. "I'm pretty wrecked, if you want to know the truth."

"The truth?" Sal bit back a sarcastic comment. Her confidence had been diminished by the long wait to hear

146

from him. At the moment she felt frazzled, confused. The bustle of the city, which had seemed so fresh and charming in the early morning hours, had worn off, and she couldn't wait to get home.

"I just got in a little while ago," he went on. "There was a big bash up in Montreal. A bunch of us flew up."

A bunch of us flew up? Sal felt a numbness growing along her shoulders, then inching down her spine as he explained about his late-night adventures. A bunch of us? Wasn't that perhaps just a euphemism for the two of us?

"It was business, Sal," he explained with a touch of impatience, as if she had accused him of something.

Well, wasn't it always? she thought. Sal steered her mind away from the offending implications. Did it really matter if he had been with another woman? She was having difficulty focusing on his explanation. It occurred to her he was adept at lying. He'd contrived another story once, because he thought she would prefer that to the truth.

"There was a lot of drinking," he elaborated. "There always is at these huge affairs. Everyone starts tossing them down in order to keep up the jolly front. Well, you know as well as I do how it's done. I didn't get back to my hotel till two."

"I'm sorry I came," Sal replied after a moment. "I don't suppose it matters if I believe you or not, Robert. What matters is that I feel completely cut off from you. I feel helpless."

"I'd like to see you." Robert's voice was suddenly hushed, as if the weariness had finally overtaken him. "I'll be there in twenty minutes."

Before she could protest, he hung up. She watched a stream of dignified businessmen approach the main desk to register. Probably here on some convention, she

147

mused. Their faces were, without exception, stern, impassive, and their eyes held that detached, far-off look she saw so often in Robert.

She ran her hands through her hair with a sense of foreboding. They were both too tired for a confrontation. She held back a tear. This was no time to indulge in self-pity or remorse. It was also no time for a conversation. Maybe he had been telling the truth, she thought. But she realized she was far too vulnerable now—the best thing she could do was to leave. Fast!

Decency, politeness, and the smallest shred of hope dictated that she should at least leave him a note. She dug in her purse for a pen and scrawled a message on a piece of hotel stationery:

I'll see you in Blue Mills. There is too much at stake to talk now.
Love, Sal.

She left it at the desk in case he came looking for her.

She was sitting in the airport lounge near the Piedmont desk when she saw him striding toward the automatic glass doors outside the terminal.

"Damn!" She had half a notion to run, to hide in the ladies' room, to do anything in order to avoid seeing him.

Once inside, he looked around with eaglelike intensity. There would be no point in hiding. She could tell by the look on his face that he was determined. He would find her even if it meant turning the airport upside down or flying back to Charlottesville on Piedmont Airlines.

She gathered her things and headed for the check-in desk, preferring to give the impression that she had seen him first.

"That was quick." She came up behind him and caught him off-guard.

He wheeled around, his eyes like bright daggers, which took her breath away. Before she could even think, he took her in his arms and kissed her with frenzied urgency.

"Robert!" She tried to protest but there was an exhilarating vehemence to his kisses which banished all thoughts of propriety.

Finally they parted and stood staring at each other, oblivious to the few passengers straggling toward the gate.

"I'm coming with you." His voice was still hoarse, and the fatigue swept over him again suddenly.

"I'll take care of your ticket," Sal said. Robert did not argue. She headed for the ticket counter, charged the ticket to her credit card, and returned to the waiting area to find him asleep.

When they announced the flight to Charlottesville he roused himself just enough to walk on board, zombie-like. He instantly collapsed into his seat and fell back asleep.

That she never questioned him about his decision to return to his cabin by the stream, nor to probe into the state of his business affairs, surprised her, until she realized she had come to accept his fitful obsessiveness by observing his commitment to his battery operated car. That his commitment, she realized, was really no different from her own commitment to painting and to the farm.

Because of her realization, Sal and Robert drifted in a newfound euphoria over the next two weeks. The same exhilarating vehemence she had tasted in his kisses at the airport now dominated their lovemaking. Sometimes he would awaken her during the night, his body throbbing with an overwhelmingly powerful virility. Often he awakened her early, stroking her flanks or nuzzling fervently against her breasts. He followed her to her special spot beside the stream, watched her paint, and then took her willingly behind some fiery sumac on a bed of dry crackling leaves. The sensuality dominating their lives was flagrant, as outrageous as the autumnal colors, and as poignant.

But the illusion of perfection which had existed during the summer was absent now that there was a real chill in the air. She felt his need for her, felt it fiercely. At the same time, the words of adoration had dried up. They might laugh with Skip and Martha, walk home hand in hand in the moonlight, and she might dream, for a moment, that he would again whisper his love for her. But it never happened. Now that she felt his love physically, she felt somehow bereft, as if a part of him had left her far behind. It was difficult to hold her peace, but she was determined.

"We're going backpacking," she announced one evening when he drove over to take her out to dinner. "No arguments."

Robert rubbed his hand over his stubbly beard and laughed. "It's too cold. That's a summer vice."

Sal made a face at him. "Abe rounded up a tent and an extra sleeping bag. Fifty degrees is hardly cold. I know people who camp out in Maine in the winter."

"They're nuts." Robert shook his head.

"We leave at five tomorrow morning." Sal grinned. "And I'm going to do all the cooking."

"It'll be the first time," he teased her.

"I bought prime steaks and a pound of potato salad."

"You call that cooking?" He laughed.

"The steaks are raw." She threw him a come-hither

glance. "They have to be cooked. I'm going to cook them. I call *that* cooking!"

As luck would have it, the day dawned gray and bleak, with a hint of frost covering the ground for the first time. Sal girded herself for Robert's protests, but apparently he had resigned himself. Or maybe—she watched him shift his Mercedes into second as it climbed another steep incline, toward the highest peak in the Shenandoahs—maybe he was already planning on checking into a hotel somewhere.

She grinned at him as he locked the trunk of the car and hoisted his backpack onto his shoulders. He was wearing an old, faded green army jacket and fatigues from the local army and navy store. With his face smoothly shaven and his black hair slicked carefully back, he looked like he'd just stepped off the page of some male-fashion layout.

"Why are you laughing?" He slipped his arm around her waist as they headed for the narrow trail which plunged through the dense forest to the river below.

"No matter what you put on," Sal scooted ahead of him as the trail narrowed, "you look fashionable. I mean, you look *right* . . . as if you were creating a fashion, setting a trend."

Robert swatted her playfully on the behind. "You're saying I'm a clotheshorse."

Sal laughed. "Something like that!"

Their laughter echoed in the vast autumnal silence, but gradually they, too, grew silent, and spoke only in whispers. The leaves crackled beneath their feet and the smell of rain permeated the air. It occurred to Sal that they really should turn back. This was scarcely the brilliant October outing she had envisioned.

Yet it had its own fragile beauty, and because of the

near-certainty of an impending storm, they were virtually the only people tramping through the state park.

Halfway down, the trail was washed out. They forded a trickling narrow tributary by balancing on slippery rocks till they reached dry land. Robert gave her hand a meaningful squeeze and she was sure he was going to suggest they turn back. Instead he motioned for her to sit next to him on a fallen tree, took an apple from his jacket pocket, and handed it to her.

Sal bit into the tart apple, feeling its juice fill her mouth, relishing the fresh crisp taste which was so like the air. She met Robert's eyes and they were locked in a primeval moment. She handed the apple to him and watched his smooth white teeth cut into the crimson skin. Her pulse accelerated wildly as he chewed, savoring the freshness as she had. His dark eyes caressed her as he held the apple out for her to take another bite.

They finished the apple in the same breathtakingly sensual silence. Around them the leaves scuttled as a pair of squirrels scampered behind a nearby tree, just in case a morsel came their way. She leaned against Robert, her face tilted toward a patch of gray sky. The air was even heavier now and a mist was beginning to form, making a fuzzy halo around the tops of the golden-leaved oaks.

Robert pulled her to her feet and without saying anything led the way. For the next hour there was only the sound of their feet scattering leaves as they descended. Once, Sal spotted a doe and a fawn, but by the time she had signaled Robert by squeezing his hand, the two creatures had leaped into the brush. She smiled at Robert and he nodded, understanding completely what had happened. Next time, his eyes seemed to say, and when he proceeded she noted a new alertness in his gait, as if he were now on the lookout for more deer.

As they reached the river bed, the wind kicked up and a few warning drops showered down on them. Sal gave him a questioning look, which he returned with an enigmatic smile as he slipped out of his backpack. She watched as he began to assemble the small tent.

"Robert." After several minutes she tapped him lightly on the shoulder. "I think there's going to be a storm. Maybe all day . . . with high winds."

He stopped in mid-movement, his eyes wide and incredulous. "You're not suggesting . . . ?"

Sal kicked at him playfully, knowing that he intended to razz her mercilessly about their thwarted outing.

"The tent is waterproof, right?" He went back to setting up the canvas.

"Right." Sal laughed. "You've made your point. If we start back now we might not get too drenched."

"And this"—he muttered as he whipped the tent into position and began staking it—"this from the girl who camps in sub-zero temperatures for days on end?"

"I never said that." She stood with her hands on her hips, watching him. Most people had a devil of a time setting up a tent for the first time. Robert was throwing it together like an Eagle Scout.

"Are you sure you've never been camping?"

"What a question?" Robert helped her out of her pack and threw both bundles inside. "Let's get our wood together."

"Robert, it's going to rain!"

He chucked her under the chin. "Are you saying you can't build a fire in the rain? Sal, you've misrepresented yourself. I trusted you!"

He started running and she chased him. The drops were larger now, though it was far from the steady downpour she envisioned. She lost sight of him, and stood looking around, waiting for him to dart out from behind a tree. He was bluffing, she thought. Once it started raining he would reveal his true intentions. She ran forward until her cheeks were stinging and red and her heart was pounding with anticipation, waiting for him to jump out at her.

But he was nowhere in sight. Like the deer, he had magically vanished into the forest.

A twig snapped and she rushed ahead, sure that she had finally found him. She felt bubbly, and trembling with an almost erotic suspense, as if this new game of his were a new prelude. Her eyes danced vibrantly as she crept stealthily forward, straining to hear a telltale rustle. She would not give in and call to him. No, she would outwait him, outguess him at his game. After several more failed attempts she began to gather dry twigs. When her arms were loaded she returned to the tent and put them inside.

She wheeled around expecting to see him grinning at her like the Cheshire cat. But his game was more complex than that, so she continued gathering wood, stacking some inside the tent where it would remain dry and building a small fire with the rest. The fire hissed when she lit it, but on the third try she coaxed a respectable blaze, added some large, well-dried logs, and balanced her old charred camping coffee pot on a rock. The lull in the precipitation would give the fire a chance to establish itself. If it wasn't a deluge, she might well be able to keep it going.

Sal sat just inside the opening to the tent and stared into the flames, feeling an enormous sense of accomplishment. During her college years she had backpacked up and down the East Coast. Robert could tease her all he liked, she thought, but at one point she had been a hell of a camper!

Robert. She closed her eyes and smiled lazily as the

logs sputtered. He never failed to amaze her. She had been certain he would leap at the chance to retreat into the dry luxury of some country inn. He seemed not only to be enjoying himself, but to be finding something deeply positive in their dampened outing.

She liked that he had challenged her, going off on his own, leaving her to build a fire—leaving her to her own thoughts for a while. She liked knowing he was out there in the woods, perhaps sniffing the smoke from her fire, listening to the birds.

By the time the coffee had perked there was a steady, faint drizzle, just enough to make the fire hiss and smoke, not enough to quench it. Sal poured herself a cup. She was sipping it when Robert appeared with his arms loaded with wood.

"You're intending to stay, I see." She smiled up at him and made room for him to sit next to her.

"It's so much better in the rain." He held his tin cup between his hands. "Did you plan this rain, Sal?"

"I can't take credit for the work of the Almighty."

"I've never been camping." He put his arm around her shoulder as he talked. "My life was stickball, and when we could afford it, a ticket to go see the Yankees play. One year my older brother was in the Fresh Air program. You know what that is?"

Sal nodded. "Where some family takes an underprivileged kid to stay with them in the country for a few weeks in the summer."

"That's right." Robert nodded. "Sounds great, right? Only my brother was terrified. My parents had to go up and get him the third night. He was afraid of the night sounds, the trees oppressed him, and he must have seen spooks behind every bush. He returned with absolutely frightening tales of life in the woods. I was seven. I believed everything he said, and you know something?

155

Until today, part of me really thought that I might get out here and experience all those scary feelings I had when I was seven. It wasn't that I was afraid—I was afraid I might be."

"Well"—Sal stroked his hand—"you've been working up to this, Robert. You've been living in the woods for nearly a month, going for long walks."

"But I have a telephone and I can always lock my door."

"Funny, I've always felt safer outside," Sal mused. "Like when I first moved into the farmhouse all by myself, I was very apprehensive, as if I might be trapped inside. I was afraid of intruders. When I'm outside, who can intrude?"

"I love your logic!" Robert chuckled softly then poked her in the ribs and pointed off to the right, where three deer were advancing toward the river. They watched in transfixed silence from under the tent as the graceful creatures lowered their slender necks to drink. Then, although neither of them had made the slightest sound or motion, one of the deer looked up, startled.

Sal's body tensed and she held her breath, willing the creatures to linger. She sensed the same reaction from Robert. They sat that way, mute and unmoving, watching the deer for what they later realized was the better part of the afternoon.

"I've never seen anything like that." Robert spoke in a whisper even after the deer had retreated back into the woods.

"Nor do I imagine you've ever sat still for that long!" Sal snuggled against him.

"Your paintings are good, Sal. You ought to do something about them."

"What brought that on?" Sal twisted her neck and looked up at him.

"This . . ." He swept his arm out to encompass the golden-hued trees muted by the light drizzle.

"I think you're prejudiced," Sal remarked. "Although in all honesty I confess I looked at some galleries in New York and by comparison I'm not half bad."

"Hmmm." Robert lapsed into reflective silence.

"What do you want, Sal?" he asked after a few minutes. "What do you really want?"

"This," she said softly. "This is what I want. It's all I really need."

"You mean living here?" Robert's voice was a low rumble against her ear, which was pressed to his chest.

Sal nodded. "Coming back here was the most crucial decision I've ever made. It was hard to leave so much . . . success, for lack of a better word, behind."

"You mean you were torn?"

"Sure I was. Not to mention the fact that everyone around me thought I was nuts for leaving Chicago."

"But you have your painting. You left because of that." He spoke the words faintly, as if he were making the statement to himself.

Sal did not reply. She stared out at the rain, which was coming down harder now. What she had said was true. This was all she needed. Only now, *this* included him. She smiled softly. The realization did not upset her. She had never needed anyone before, and now, for the first time, she yielded to the knowledge that she needed him.

"I love you. . . ." She climbed to her knees and framed his face between her palms.

"I'm not a very good risk." Robert met her eyes candidly.

"I know," she said as she smiled and returned to her position, cradled in his arms.

157

"I was thinking of taking my children on a camping trip," he said unexpectedly.

"That's a good idea." Sal closed her eyes, lulled by the rain. "Will you take them to Maine, in winter? Have I unleashed a wilderness freak by prodding you into this outing?"

Robert wrapped his arms tighter around her. "No, I wasn't thinking of Maine. I'm not a masochist. There are limits. I'll leave the ice fishing to you. I was thinking more like St. John in the Virgin Islands. I want to have all four children together. They hardly know each other. Being out here with you makes me realize how sad that is. They have different mothers, different lives, they live in different parts of the world. But I would like to show them something I've never been able to show, something that's impossible to show at another dinner in a fancy restaurant where everyone is on good behavior and playing at having a good time. I don't know if I can make up for my lack of paternal expertise, but for the first time I think I see a way of trying."

"Can I come?" Sal uttered the question without hesitation.

"Yes." Robert gathered her up in his arms and kissed her tenderly.

During all of their intimate moments Sal had never felt such closeness between them. Well into evening they sat huddled together, drinking coffee and talking. For the first time Robert spoke at length about his failed marriages, about his compulsion to succeed, his rigidity, and his almost obsessive drive to make money—not so much out of a desire to be wealthy as out of some deeply rooted necessity to prove that he could do it.

Sal spoke of her family, of the pressure she had felt to be the one successful Carter in a family of dirt farmers. For the first time she invited him home to meet her parents, and his enthusiasm gratified her more than she would have thought possible.

"What about those steaks?" Robert taunted her with a grin as he lit the kerosene lamp. The rain had been beating down on the tent for over an hour, and there wasn't the least chance that the fire was still going.

"Outfoxed." Sal stretched out on her sleeping bag and yawned.

"Saved by the rain!" Robert lay down beside her and slipped his hand under her sweater to caress her breast.

Sal wriggled against his seductive fingers as they gently squeezed one nipple.

"Why didn't I think of this sooner?" Robert's mouth was warm and coaxing. His tongue slipped expertly inside, swirling and delving deeper, making her flush and grow hot with desire.

She returned his devilish thrusts, her passion building as his hand manipulated her bare breast and swept down her lean torso to the button on her jeans. She sucked in her stomach as he unzipped her jeans. She was already drenched in desire for him, and as his hand plunged lower into that fair thicket, she was seized by a devastating impatience.

"We have all night," he murmured, but that did nothing to assuage the agony of her desire. Her hands grasped his haunches then raced to unfasten his belt. His fingers were alive inside her, dancing like the slicing rain, propelling her into sensual oblivion.

He wriggled out of his jeans, tore off his shirt, and bent to remove her jeans. His body was like fire, smooth and lean beneath her fingers. He was primed and she experienced again the awe, the wonder at the magnificence of his staunch virility. The lamp cast warm, erotic shadows on the inside of their tent, and in that rosy light he had never seemed more beautiful.

"Sal . . ." He crouched over her, his face eager and strangely young. Tonight he possessed a new vitality that far surpassed his usual dynamic energy. She ran her hand along his rib cage and shuddered in delight at the sensation of his flesh, his bones, all of him. She traced her forefinger down the line of wiry hair and covered him, relishing the pulsating sensation inside her palm. He weaved from side to side as she caressed him, and then, unable to endure her warmly prodding fingers, he assumed control. With unerring mastery he possessed her, like lightning and like rain he was filling her.

This was the beginning. A new world for them, a day filled with surprises, a night brimming with mystery. His legs were like iron wound around her as he propelled her onto her side. She felt possessed by his sinewy body at every angle, felt his muscular power as a force as potent and furious as the wind which howled outside the tent.

She was being tossed, pitched about, hurled into a red-hot churning sea. Her body was wracked by a series of convulsions which left her gasping. When he rolled her over she assumed control, striking her own scintillating rhythm, driving him mercilessly, then pulling back. When he cried out suddenly, she raced to join him, feeling no greater satisfaction, no greater happiness from anything than from the look of deep contentment on his flushed face.

He sighed and closed his eyes, smiling. The storm shook the tent, and although the temperature had dropped, it was steamy warm inside. The fragrance of love filled the air, and as she snuggled against his shoulder she knew that this would be a long night of love, perhaps a night that would go on forever.

CHAPTER TEN

A week later, having spent the entire day in her studio painting, Sal peeked in on Abe, who was at work at his easel.

"What's new?" She stood smiling in the doorway.

"I should ask you the same." Abe stood back and grimaced at a glob of cerulean blue.

"Robert's in New York."

"Things going well between you?" Abe dabbed some turpentine on a cloth and smeared out the glob.

"Yes." Sal beamed.

"I see in the papers he's come up with a new investor. Once a figure gets beyond seven numbers I phase out. He's come up with a lot of money to get the ball rolling on his car again."

"Don't ask me how he did it." Sal raised her hands in authentic disbelief. "He's spent most of his time down here. I guess when he decides to do something, it happens."

"Hmmm." Abe was circumspect.

"You still don't like him." Sal moved across the room and perched on a stool next to the painting.

"It doesn't matter." Abe made a feeble attempt at sounding convinced.

"You're my best friend," Sal said. "It matters."

Abe shrugged. "Maybe I'm jealous."

"Jealous?" Sal exclaimed.

"I don't mean sexually," Abe amended quickly. "I mean, I've hardly seen anything of you since he took up residence in Blue Mills. I feel like I've lost you."

Sal frowned. She knew precisely what he meant. She'd been feeling the same way herself. True, things with Robert had blossomed lately and she felt genuinely close to him. But she was also beginning to feel isolated. The only people they saw were Martha and Skip.

"Come to dinner Saturday night," she suggested. Then, in response to his doubtful expression she added brightly, "Don't look that way, Abe. There's a first time for everything. I'll cook something. And bring Dorie. If we have an evening together—"

"Dorie and I have split," Abe interjected evenly.

"What?" Sal bolted off the stool. "You didn't say anything!"

"We haven't had a chance to talk," Abe said simply.

"When . . . why . . . what happened?"

"I want something more permanent. She's not sure."

"I'm sorry." Sal reached out and took his arm. "But she loves you, Abe. I know she does."

"I know it too." Abe shook his head, looking depressed.

"Bad timing." Abe roused himself. "That's all. Sometimes things don't work because the timing's off."

"But if two people love each—" Sal broke off, suddenly aware that she was thinking of herself, speaking of herself and Robert as much as Abe and Dorie. Since

Robert's mention of marriage early in their relationship, the subject had not come up, except for him to point out that he was a bad risk.

"It'll work out." Sal feigned a confidence she was not sure she believed. "Damn it, Abe, it has to!"

Two hours later Sal was back in her studio painting furiously—mainly, she realized, to relieve the tensions which had erupted as the result of her conversation with Abe. As in the old days, they were each closeted away in their separate studios, with Beethoven blaring and shaking the rafters in the old house.

Well, at least she was doing something constructive by painting, Sal thought, instead of fantasizing about all of the negative things that might wedge a gap between her and Robert. She shouted out a word of encouragement to Abe over the robust symphony. After all, Robert had asked her to go camping with his children, she mused. That was something.

But she knew there was much that was tenuous in their life together. Now that his company was solvent again, he would soon be busy in its behalf. As winter approached, the prospect of seeing less and less of him was almost a fait accompli.

As she painted she chided herself for worrying, for her lack of confidence. After all, he'd only been gone two days, she noted. She paused with her brush midair and looked around her cluttered studio. Completed canvases lined the walls, and some of them—even she had to admit—were good. The fall had been an extraordinarily productive period.

Sal returned to her work in progress, which was a departure from the richly textured landscapes she had been painting. Since the camping trip, she had gone indoors, as Robert liked to say. She had assembled an eclectic array of articles—a fragile, etched perfume bottle; a perfectly round pumpkin; an old pair of long, white formal gloves; and a large, rusty, and quite lethal-looking butcher knife—all of which she arranged on a stunning piece of delicate lace. Robert teased her that she was being purposefully obscure with her still life, but the more she worked on the painting the more intrigued she was with her choices. Tonight, with Beethoven blasting away, she worked tirelessly, losing sight of the time until a creak in her neck prompted her to consult her watch.

"Abe!" she called out over the music. "It's nearly two o'clock. I'll rustle up some eggs if you'll eat them."

"Twenty more minutes," came Abe's muffled reply.

She smiled and returned to her painting with renewed vigor. The work had cleansed her, as it often did. It was important to keep things straight, she thought. She and Robert were not Dorie and Abe, and just because they were having difficulties didn't mean there were problems ahead for her.

Just as she was about to call it quits, a car's lights beamed into the room. For an instant the old fear clutched at her heart, but then she reminded herself she wasn't alone. She dashed to the window in time to see Robert slam the car door shut and stride purposefully onto the porch.

At two o'clock in the morning? she thought. A new fear ran through her. He wasn't due back for several days, or at least that was his projection when he left. Could there have been another economic calamity? she wondered.

Sal shot out of her studio, shouting news of Robert's arrival to Abe as she passed his door. Beethoven was still resounding through the house and she nearly collided with Robert, who was already on his way upstairs.

"What happened?" Her voice was filled with alarm as she reached for him.

He gave her a hard look, jerked his arm away, and continued up the stairs.

"Robert, what's the matter? Tell me. Did something—"

She watched him pass Abe's doorway and move on down the hall to their bedroom. Heart pounding, she followed him and closed the door.

"You weren't due back until the weekend. What is it?" A tentative note crept into her voice as she read the anger in his face.

"Why don't you just come out with it, Sal? You're always preaching honesty at any cost."

"I don't know what you're talking about." Sal girded herself for battle. It had been weeks since he had complained about Abe's presence. At the time, because Robert himself was spending so much time at the house, she had conceded that Abe's random in-and-out-at-all-hours behavior should be mitigated somewhat.

"It's two in the morning," Robert said pointedly, as if that fact cinched his point and justified his anger.

"I don't care if it's six in the morning, or three, or what time it is!" Sal retorted hotly.

"Seeing him makes me wonder what goes on when I'm not here."

"Don't be ridiculous." Sal cautioned herself not to respond to his pugnaciousness. It was bad enough that he didn't care for Abe, she thought—that he was still somehow threatened because of her closeness with another man.

"Robert, something is bothering you. Don't try to project it onto something I did. Abe is my friend, but that's all. I've told you that before but you persist in your archaic interpretation of the way things *must* be between a man and a woman."

"We agreed that he would confine his hours here to a more . . ."

". . . respectable schedule." Sal could not resist completing his thought.

"Yes." Robert ignored her sarcasm.

"But you're not here," Sal argued. "Why does it matter? Are you really concerned about appearances? Who's going to see?"

"It's not right." Robert's anger gave way to bewilderment.

"What are you saying?" Sal felt her impatience grow. Was he really that conventional? she wondered. Was he trying to groom her now for a more acceptable lifestyle? Or was he jealous of the relaxed, uncomplicated relationship she had with Abe? She had thought that in time he would come to respect if not value and like Abe because of the closeness between them. Abe was her best friend. She had explained that to Robert countless times, but he remained skeptical. If Abe had been a woman, she was certain Robert would have made more of an effort to understand why she loved him.

"How late does he stay, Sal?"

Sal shook her head in disbelief. "You think you caught me in some act of indiscretion. You can't think that!"

She reached out for him but he held her off.

"Sal, in case you haven't noticed, my name manages to make the headlines from time to time. Some of my investors are rather conservative. . . ."

"And you're saying that I have to watch how I act because of your business reputation?"

"That's not what I said." Robert frowned.

"I think you're the one who is conservative," Sal said

in a restrained voice. "You think it's all right for Abe to be here as long as the sun is out."

"Don't be sarcastic." Robert gave her a sideways glance. "A lot of people, most people, would say the same thing."

"But I'm not most people and neither are you." Sal faced him squarely. "I don't live my life according to the clock. In case you've forgotten, I gave all that up."

"It's this completely offbeat life-style of yours," he said with an accusing tone.

"I'm an artist." Sal recoiled at the implication. "I don't have time to polish the silver. I don't even have time to buy the silver. I don't even want to own silver! I've tried to tell you—I want *time,* time to do what I want to do, and if that means painting all night with another artist—male or female—then I'll do it!"

"No structure, right? You want a completely unstructured, anarchic life? What about children and family responsibilities?"

Sal gaped at him. Why was he getting into this now? she wondered. It had been ages since he'd mentioned marriage. Was he trying to tell her that unless she changed her bohemian ways she would not be a suitable wife? Is that why the subject of marriage had never come up again?

"I never tried to hide anything from you, Robert," she told him. "You knew the kind of woman I was the first day we met. You knew I'd left that nine-to-five, cocktail-party life behind, and you knew I wanted no part of playing at projecting the right image. What you're trying to say is you can't imagine me and any friends I might have at your fancy fund-raising parties."

"Sal, that's an exaggeration. You're perfectly capable of making an impression on people."

"But I don't want to make an impression!" Sal shouted. "I just want to be me."

"And that includes having a lover on the side?" Robert asked in a voice as gentle as death.

"What!" Sal exploded again. "How many times do I have to tell you? Why don't you trust me?"

"He practically lives here, Sal. I'm not blind. I see the way he looks at you."

"What you see is someone who cares for me! That is what you see. But I'll tell you something, Robert. You are blind!"

Sal raised her voice above the crescendo in Beethoven's Fifth. "Abe uses two rooms here for studios because he doesn't have enough space in his little postage-stamp cabin. I'll tell you what I think—I think you resent him for living like a pauper, for doing what he wants to do . . . for being poor but free. Yes, I never thought of it till now, but I think Abe's presence reminds you that you are somehow missing out on something. And maybe you don't have as much nerve as he does. Maybe if you gave up all of your other business ventures and concentrated solely on the car, you'd be able to solve the problems. But that would be risky, wouldn't it? It might mean giving up too much prestige."

"You don't know what you're talking about!" Robert glared at her.

"Maybe I don't." She turned away from him, shaking with rage.

"I guess I just don't understand this helter-skelter existence you live." Robert looked around Sal's topsy-turvy room. When he was around she made an effort at organization. But in his absence her mind was elsewhere, and generally the domestic side of her life deteriorated considerably.

"You've always known that about me." Sal stood stiffly, staring out the window, her arms hanging limply at her side. The final notes of the symphony resounded, then the house was silent.

She was thinking of the night she had flown to New York, and the following day, when he had finally phoned. She had never once accused him, had never once let her insecurities spill over into suspicious, petty accusations.

"I wish you'd be reasonable." She fought the rising tide of emotion and spoke in a cool voice.

In the silence she could feel him withdraw. She no longer cared why he had decided to return at this ungodly hour. She felt exhausted, defeated. It was finally clear to her that marriage or not, a life with Robert Capolla would limit her freedom too much.

She turned to him slowly. "You may own this house, Robert, but you can't come waltzing in here like the lord of the manor and throw a tantrum because something seems wrong."

"All I'm asking is that he doesn't spend the night here—when I'm here, or when I'm away. I don't think that's a lot to ask."

"I'm appalled at your provincial thinking," she cried. "You don't own me now and you never will."

"You've made that clear often enough." Robert turned and walked out of the bedroom.

Sal stood rooted to the floor. She watched him walk down the porch steps and get into his car. Her hands were numb with fury. She wanted to raise the window and hurl invectives at him, or fling some sharp object at his silver Mercedes, which seemed to glow in the moonlight. She watched the car disappear down the lane and then exploded in a roar that shook the house as the Beethoven had shaken it earlier.

"What is it?" Abe loped into her bedroom, concerned and wide-eyed.

"Him!" Sal clenched and unclenched her fists. She began pacing around the room like a tigress.

"I heard voices." Abe watched her from a distance.

"I bet," Sal fumed. "I hate him. I really hate him!"

"You want to talk . . . ?"

Sal shook her head vehemently. "A waste of time. I just want to forget."

Abe reached out to her, but she shrugged him off.

"I'm all right! Honestly. I don't think I'm up for those eggs though. Maybe a glass of warm milk and then I'm going to sleep."

But Sal couldn't sleep, and the next morning she staggered through her chores like a zombie. The only thing that saved her was her anger. Every time she thought of Robert Capolla, her hands clenched themselves into hard fists and an overwhelming urge to start slugging something came over her. When she went in for her midmorning cup of coffee, the phone was ringing. She felt a moment's excitement but dismissed it. She resolved not to be taken in by him again. At heart he was a man with limited vision, she thought, jealous and possessive. He had failed at two marriages, and should he opt for a third, he would fail at that too. How dare he allude to her bohemian existence, she fumed, and to her domestic laxity: It was none of his business. She rented his house, she wasn't his housekeeper.

She was relieved she'd kept that end of it straight. He had wanted her to go on living here rent free but she had declined, and now she experienced some small satisfaction at least in that. She was not beholden to him in any way, she reasoned, and never would be. She saw him now as a man who would wield his gifts as a form of power.

Though Sal did not feel like painting, she forced herself to spend the afternoon at the easel. Abe kept popping in to make sure she was all right, but he knew her well enough to know it was futile to try and get her to talk if she didn't feel like it.

At six that evening she stuck her head into his studio and suggested they drive into town to go to a movie. As she dressed she wished perversely that Robert would see her and Abe together. She told herself she no longer cared what he thought, that she would just as soon have him think the worst.

After the movie they went for a beer, both of them mopey-eyed and reticent.

"Some pair, huh?" Abe walked her to her car around midnight.

"I'm thinking of taking a trip," she said tightly as she climbed into her station wagon. "I need to get away. I'm driving to Chicago . . . maybe even tonight."

"Sal, be sensible." Abe looked alarmed. "Listen, I know how you feel."

"I have to get away." Sal's eyes flashed with fury. The anger was feeding her. She felt as if she could drive for two days straight without sleeping.

"I've paid the rent through December," she said. "I want you to use the house." She pressed a key into his hand. "I'll have the phone disconnected before I leave. I'll be back by Thanksgiving."

By the time she crossed over into West Virginia the numbness was wearing off. In place of the anger a sick, dismal feeling, unlike anything she had ever known, swept over her. In a daze she pulled off the road at the sight of the first motel, checked into a tourist cabin, and fell into bed. When she woke it was already dark again.

Her watch had stopped but she calculated she had slept over twenty-four hours.

Sal knew she wasn't herself. She felt like someone else, like someone without hope. She staggered out of bed, undressed, and stood under a scalding shower. She stepped out of the shower and fell back into bed. The next morning she was hungry. Considering this a positive sign, she checked out of the motel, ate an enormous breakfast, and turned the car around and headed back to Blue Mills.

She would not think of Robert Capolla. Every time his name or his image threatened to intrude, she steered her mind elsewhere. By the time she turned up the driveway, Sal was on fire with a new determination, the same brand of determination that had enabled her to leave Chicago in the first place.

There was an uncommon chill in the house when she entered but she dismissed it, and taking the stairs two at a time, went into her room and put on a warm sweater. Automatically she reached for the phone. Remembering she had ordered it disconnected, she made a mental note to drive over to her parents' when she finished her evening chores. She would also have to phone Wendell, she thought, and tell him she had returned earlier than expected so he wouldn't have to feed the cattle before going to school in the morning.

Feeling like a miracle of efficiency, she vacuumed the house and went back outside to check the livestock. Everything was fine, she thought: She had trained Wendell well—he could be counted on. When she was settled into her own place, she mused, she would hire him on a permanent basis, perhaps even cut him in on a percentage of profits, in order to give him greater incentive.

Sal toyed with the idea of driving over to Abe's. She

172

had expected to find him in his studio, but judging from the canvas on the easel, he hadn't been there in several days. Instead she elected to hike over to Skip and Martha's around dusk.

She could tell by the discreet way Martha greeted her that the elderly couple had learned the details of her sudden departure from Abe. They cautiously skirted any reference to Robert, and were just as careful not to be too solicitous.

Back in her bed, she finished devouring one of her mysteries and fell asleep.

Awakened in the middle of the night by the crunch of gravel, Sal gritted her teeth, lying absolutely still. She knew perfectly well who it was. Well, she had locked all the doors, she thought. If he had the audacity to use another key, she decided, she would press charges.

Sal broke out in a cold sweat at the sound of his hammering on the door. She was livid, her anger back full-blown, and it took every ounce of control to lie there in silence.

Finally he left, having utterly destroyed the equilibrium she had struggled so hard to find. Sal bolted from her bed, flung on her old flannel robe, and went into the studio. She was still painting at seven thirty the next morning when Abe came in.

"Skip and Martha called." He looked at her haggard face with a sympathetic smile.

"I figured they would." She gave up all pretense and sank back into a chair.

"Sal, Robert called before they took the phone out."

Sal gave a heavy sigh. "I'm sorry if it was unpleasant."

"Not for me it wasn't. He just asked where you were and I told him. He seemed upset."

"Too bad," Sal said tightly.

"You should at least talk to him, Sal. I don't know what went on between the two of you but—"

"He was threatened by your late-night presence in my house," she said listlessly.

"I was afraid of that." Abe hung his head dismally, as if he were entirely to blame. "Why don't I talk to him?"

"No!" Sal exploded. "No, you have nothing to explain and neither do I. I don't need to justify things to him. I don't want to be involved with a man who wants to run my life and dictate whom I can and cannot see. You are my dearest friend. You will be welcome in my home at any hour of the day or night! Amen!"

Abe looked relieved by her spunky outburst. "Thanks."

"How are things with Dorie?" she asked him.

"We're together again."

"Oh, Abe, that's great." She perked up.

"If we can work it out, maybe you can too." He saw that she didn't want to talk about Robert anymore so he changed the subject. "You also had a phone call from that real estate agent who showed you the property you were interested in. Apparently the owner has lowered the asking price and is willing to finance the mortgage herself. He called the day you left. They took the phone out right after that. Luckily it was still connected, Sal."

"Yeah." Sal nodded distractedly. "Yeah, that was lucky. I'd better drive right over and make sure I didn't miss out on it."

She hopped to her feet and started out of the room. Suddenly she stopped and put her hand over her mouth to stifle a sob. The tears spilled out hot and heavy, and when Abe put his arms around her she sobbed harder.

"Sal, you're a woman who gets what she wants. I gather Capolla is a man who gets what he wants too. As a strictly prejudiced onlooker, I'd have to say you two

174

were well suited. If there's anyone who can get what she wants, it's you. If you want him, you'll find a way to bring him around. I know you will."

With Abe's words echoing in her ears, Sal went into her room and dressed. Without making a conscious decision, she dressed carefully in a pair of brown tweed slacks, which were gathered softly at the waist, a white cashmere sweater, and a brown leather jacket. As she leaned toward the mirror to put on the delicate gold-drop earrings Robert had given her, she caught sight of her face, more lively than it had been for days.

Later that morning Ben Higgins, the real estate agent who had first showed her the property, welcomed her with a firm handshake. It was true, he said, the owner of the property had indeed lowered her asking price and was willing to finance it at an unbelievably low nine percent.

"What's the catch?" Sal could scarcely believe her ears. No one could get a nine-percent mortgage these days.

"No catch." Ben lit his pipe and puffed contentedly. "Winter's comin' on and the old gal's got her eye on some trailer park in Florida. Needs the cash."

"Then it's a floating mortgage?" Sal wracked her brain to think of possible loopholes in the deal.

"No ma'am, it is not." Ben shook his head. "It's a firm nine percent, and if you put down another five thousand you can have an option on the twenty acres the other side of the stream."

"If I could find five thousand . . ." Sal scribbled some figures on a yellow legal pad as she mulled over the offer. If she sold out the remaining percentage of her business, she would be able to put money down on the option too. Then she would really have herself quite a spread, she thought.

175

"Okay, Ben." She slapped her palm down on his desk with a note of finality. "I'm writing you a check to cover the binder. Hold onto it till I transfer some money into my account at the bank. It should be good by tomorrow. I'll have to let you know about the option."

"Take your time, take your time." Ben shook her hand again then waved as she climbed back into her station wagon.

As Sal backed out to the highway, her heart was beating double time and she had to pull off again and sit for a moment, composing herself. She was actually doing it, she thought. She was no longer in the position of trying out her new life-style, she was committed.

Going for broke, she mused, that's what she was doing. Maybe it was time to go for broke as far as Robert was concerned, she thought. After all, he was the only man in her life who had ever caused her so much grief, or brought her so much joy, so much ecstasy. Maybe Abe was right. Maybe she could bring him around.

As Sal approached the turnoff to his cabin, she got cold feet, backed up, and pulled into one of the dingy little truck stops that lined this section of the highway. Insulating herself against the stares of strangers, she sat at the far end of the counter and ordered a cup of tea with lemon. Maybe he had already left for New York, she thought. Maybe his impromptu visit last night had been his last farewell. Or had he simply stopped by out of curiosity to see if Abe was, as he had said, still hanging around?

It didn't matter. She girded herself. Only fools stood on ceremony, she thought. Only a fool would turn her back on what she really wanted. And she wanted Robert Capolla, part time or full time, with marriage or without. She did not want the suffering. But that was up to her, wasn't it? she asked herself. Maybe he couldn't change. Maybe he would always be jealous. But that didn't mean she had to submit to his dictates. In the face of his accusations, she thought, she might learn to remain calm—not to turn the other cheek like a suffering-in-silence victim, but to quite honestly rise above the situation. After all, it took two to quarrel. If she hadn't felt threatened by his accusations, she mused, she might have reacted differently.

Sal rolled down the window of her station wagon and rested her arm casually on the window frame as she drove. The weather had shifted, and for a moment the bright cast of the sun and the fragrance of the almost warm breeze transported her back into summer. She should never have worn her cashmere sweater, she mused: This was a day to slip your feet into a running brook, or even shed your clothes altogether and enjoy a final exhilarating dip.

She would soon own her own spread, she thought. This knowledge brought on a state of optimism and confidence. It was still too soon to know for sure, but from the looks of her books, she was almost going to break even her first year. There was no reason to think she wouldn't do even better next year, she mused. And the more profit she realized from farming, the more she would be free to spend her time painting.

She swung the car along the dusty road to Robert's secluded cabin. Her heart accelerated wildly at the sight of his car. She turned off her ignition and sat for a moment, overcome by a dizzy, tingling sensation. Maybe it was better not to guess what would happen when she saw him, or to plan her opening remarks, which was her usual proclivity.

The house was still as she approached. She tapped lightly, and when there was no reply she called to him. She was weak with suspense, shifting from one foot to the other, her eyes darting in expectation of his sudden appearance.

Sal leaned against the door, her cheeks bright pink from the anticipation. And she was hot—too hot, she thought. She headed for the leaf-strewn trail which wound along the bank of the stream. She tried not to think, but found herself wondering what she was going to say. What did she really want?

She felt herself bubbling with fierce emotions as she followed the rushing stream. Robert was still here. That, she told herself, was a positive sign.

Finally, she spotted him slouched up against the thick trunk of a giant oak, his fishing pole propped up between his knees. At first she thought he was dozing, but as she drew closer she saw that he was sitting very still, his dark eyes focused in the middle of the stream. She tiptoed closer, reluctant to intrude, and since he gave no sign of noticing her, she paused several feet away and waited.

He jiggled the line slightly and his expression intensified as a circle of tiny bubbles marred the smooth surface of the water. She stared at the pole held loosely in his hands, and something in her quickened at the sight of his long fingers, so relaxed and sure. His hands guided the line slowly to the right. They were beautiful hands, so sensitive-looking, yet capable of authoritativeness. The reel made a faint whirring sound as he released more line. He was sitting so still now that he seemed not even to be breathing.

Suddenly the line quivered and the bobber disappeared in a circle of churning water. Robert's expression did not change. He remained unerringly calm as the line reeled out and the water grew more turbulent from the thrashing of his unseen opponent.

Sal found that she was holding her breath and that

her body had broken out in a suspenseful fever as she watched the expertise with which he slowly, ever so slowly and painstakingly, wound in a portion of the line. Again there was a horrible thrashing as the fish decided to run with it. Robert moved his left arm upward and for the first time Sal noted the tension in the strong muscles of his forearm. He only appeared to be in a state of absolute repose. In fact, his body was rigid and he was expending an incredible amount of energy controlling his responses.

There was an erotic tugging in her stomach as his arm muscle twitched and he tightened his grip on the pole. Suddenly, without warning, he whipped the line out of the water and hurled a large, flailing bass onto the bank.

The violence of the sudden gesture caught her off-guard. She felt her mouth go dry as she watched him move over to the fish. He bent down, his back to her, and for some time he held that position, his shoulders hunched forward, his hands moving rapidly as he removed the hook.

To her surprise he stood up, walked back to the stream, and holding the ten-inch bass loosely in his hands, allowed it to slither back into the stream.

He turned to her, as if he'd known she'd been there all along. "I never keep them," he said, wiping his wet hands on his jeans. His dark eyes were veiled.

Sal smiled slowly. Her palpitations had subsided and she was overwhelmed by a feeling of confidence, a sense of security about herself, Robert, and their future.

"You really have developed into some fisherman."

"I've had a lot of practice lately." Robert caught her eye for a moment, then looked away.

"You've changed, Robert," she said softly. "I can

hardly believe you're the same man who came to pay me a professional call last July."

"Is that a compliment?" Robert faced her for the first time, his eyes dark and brooding with an unmistakable erotic glint.

"It is a compliment." Sal met his eyes willingly. For the first time since meeting him, the word compromise entered her mind. Suddenly it seemed an enormously positive word. She sank down onto the bank and looked up at him. Yes, Robert *had* changed, she thought. He had grown in so many ways over the past months. She had always known that he would have to change if things were to work out, but until this instant she had never fully taken into account the ways in which she, too, might want to expand and develop.

"I don't know where to start." Her southern accent thickened, as it always did when she became emotional.

"I'll listen." He sat down next to her, still reserved, but at least willing to hear her out.

"I guess I sort of set myself up as the moral barometer between the two of us. In a way, I think it's amazing we managed to stay together this long, with all the shuttling you've done between here and New York. I reckon I've been rather narrow-minded and selfish about that . . . I mean about turning down those early offers to come with you to New York, to meet your friends and see what your life was like there. And yet the one time I flew up, I didn't even suggest staying for a few days."

"And I didn't suggest it," Robert said, "because I figured you'd turn me down. There was always the livestock to consider."

"I know." Sal sighed. "I made it hard for you, didn't I? I wasn't even aware of how hardheaded I was being."

Robert nodded, not unkindly but with an aloofness which was making her hands perspire.

"Maybe I didn't have enough confidence in myself as an artist." Sal plunged ahead, determined. "I'd always thought of New York in a negative way, as just another city. After all, I'd worked very hard to leave one city, so why on earth would I want to move to another?"

She paused for a moment, her eyes filled with love, with longing, and with a deep, urgent desire to be understood. "But there was every reason to want to spend some time there. Because you were there—your life. Because I loved . . . love you."

Robert's dark lashes fluttered briefly, but he did not look up.

"I was rigid," Sal admitted softly. "I was deaf to your telling me that as an artist there was much I could learn if I spent time in New York. Every artist needs to make contact with the creative source, and as you said, New York is the art center of—"

Sal broke off nervously, then jumped in again with greater urgency. "I don't want to lose you, Robert. The crazy thing is, I've just put a binder on a piece of property. I can't leave all this behind, but I'd like to find a way of sharing the life you have in the city too."

Robert exhaled slowly, stood up, and moved back to his fishing pole. His reticence was unexpected. He was quiet, too quiet for a man who was never at a loss for words. His response sent a chill of fear through Sal as she waited for his reply.

CHAPTER ELEVEN

Robert picked up his fishing line and fingered the hook with a tight, concentrated frown on his face. He seemed so utterly absorbed that for an instant Sal wondered if he had even heard her.

"Robert . . . ?" She strained toward him, not daring to move to his side. The heat was stifling and moist. She watched him toss his line back into the stream, wiggling it slightly so that the smooth surface of the water was marred by tiny lines.

"The Compleat Angler," he said. "Ever read it?"

Sal shook her head with a consternation.

"Izaak Walton wrote it. I forget in which century, but early. I checked it out of the university library the day Abe told me you'd left for Chicago. I understand why people become obsessed with fishing."

He cocked his head to one side, staring at the waters which were once again smooth and unruffled. "For one thing, it's a lesson in patience," he went on. "It's not like business. No, not at all. There's nothing to be done.

Except wait . . . until the fish decides to take a nibble. Some fish are smarter than others. It's the wily ones, like that bass I just pulled in, that elevate the sport to something of a philosophical pursuit."

Sal waited for him to continue but he sidestepped stealthily along the bank, moving the line deftly as he went. Was that his response to her speech? she wondered. A discourse on fishing?

After a moment she walked cautiously in his direction, being careful not to step on a twig or scuffle the leaves. She watched him with a fascinated, rapt expression.

"You say I've changed." He spoke with his back to her. "And you're right. I have. In bits and pieces."

He drew the empty line out of the water and turned to her. His dark eyes were bright with a fierce light. "After you took off for Chicago, I felt myself in a state of shock . . . shock that I, Robert Capolla, would find myself in such confusing circumstances. It wasn't what you did—that is, leave without a word. It was me. Over the summer I'd changed and I wasn't sure who I was."

Sal stared at him with a bewildered expression. He moved toward her slowly, his face now utterly composed.

"I know now that I can't continue my life as it has been."

Sal drew her brows together, feeling more and more at a loss. Was he saying that *they* couldn't continue? That they were through?

"I'm glad you want to spend some time in New York." He stopped a few feet away and looked at her evenly. "You should. For your own sake, for the sake of your work."

"And . . . that's all?" The question burst out of her. "Robert, didn't you hear me? I want to share *your* life too. It's made you what you are, it's made you the man I love as much as anything else and—damn it!"

She flushed as she rushed on. "I've been just so self-absorbed, so bent on making sure that you didn't dominate me that—"

"Well, there's nothing wrong with that, Sal," Robert said calmly. A gentle smile played on his mouth as he regarded her.

"But I went too far," Sal protested, feeling frustrated and baffled by their encounter.

"You didn't." Robert's eyes softened.

Sal caught her breath at the sensation of his nearness. They were standing a few feet apart, and there was no mistaking the fiery currents zigzagging between them.

"You didn't go too far, Sal," he repeated.

Their eyes locked in a deep, abiding look which sent erotic tremors through her body.

"I love you, Sal. I don't think I'll make a mistake with you. I don't think you'll let me."

"Robert, I'm so confused. I'm not used to double—to fancy talk. What are you saying?"

Robert grinned at her response. "I'm saying I love you. I'm saying you have no business apologizing for being the sort of woman you are. I'm saying, plain as I can, that when . . . *if* you'll marry me, it'll work to both of our advantages. I'm sure I can make you happy."

"Oh . . ." Sal's face crumpled and tears slid down her cheeks as she stared at him. "Of course you can make me happy!"

She threw her arms around his neck and hugged him with unreserved fierceness, with all the power and strength she possessed.

"Robert, I love you!" She sought his mouth with the same unbridled hunger.

184

Her body seemed to ooze with a new sensuality as her breasts flattened against his hard chest. How she loved him, she thought—yes, and how he loved her. She was sure of it. His tongue was rampant and demanding, gliding back and forth between her parted lips. She drew him in deeper, tantalizing him with soft forays, testing the fullness of his lips, relishing the sharpness of his fine white teeth.

He seemed thinner. She ran her hands along the outside of his rib cage and felt an insistent tugging in the pit of her stomach.

"I want to make love to you," he murmured.

"Yes!" Sal pressed against him, feeling her delicious erotic currents rage and swell.

Robert's hands moved deftly under her sweater, cupping her breasts. A groan of pleasure escaped from his lips as he fingered her nipples, and in one lightning-swift movement he swept the sweater up over her head and unfastened her bra.

Sal felt her nipples tighten and swell to an almost painful sensitivity as he stood back to gaze at her. He extended one hand and touched her left breast tenderly.

"We could be married here," he said thickly as he stroked her ample breast. "As soon as we can wade through the red tape. Next week at the latest."

"Yes." Sal's eyes glistened as she replied. "And live happily ever after."

Robert gave her a dazzling glance as he began recklessly tearing off his shirt.

"Here . . ." He grabbed her hand and drew her up the bank, behind a fiery sumac bush. He threw down his shirt and began stripping out of his jeans.

A sense of wild urgency was upon them as they shed their clothes and fell naked down upon the bed of crackling leaves. Robert's shirt was a paltry ground-cover, but it did not matter. Their legs wound around each other, pale against the russets and the reds. They were seared together, moving in a delirious, frenzied dance beneath the bright-blue October sky.

"How I love you!" Robert looked down into her flushed face.

A series of wild convulsions made her gasp as he glided deeper and deeper inside her. She clutched at his shoulders, urging him on, arching upward as he moved with unerring rhythm.

There was an air of complete abandon as they pulled apart and came together once again, glorying in the dizzying delights they offered each other. They rolled over in the leaves, laughing, and their bodies glistened as if they had been drenched in dew. Robert placed his hands on her bare haunches as she crouched over him, leading him off on a slow erotic rhythm of her own. He massaged her, goading her, thrusting up into her unsparingly as she danced above him. The world was whirling and the moist heat and the crackling leaves heightened all of their senses, propelling them to greater sensuality.

Another series of convulsions wracked Sal's body and she cried out in ecstasy, her throaty voice echoing through the forest. Robert pierced her with a sensual frenzy obliterating all thought, all sound. There was only his fine, hard, slippery body moving wildly above her, making her gasp and gulp and cry out again and again.

A great rumble shook his body as he gave one final exalted thrust and fell silent. For what seemed a glorious eternity they lay wrapped in each other's arms, listening to the soft gurgles of the river, the occasional song of a bird, and the constant rhythms of their pounding hearts. Finally, Robert pulled himself to a sitting

186

position and smiled down at her. She was a picture of tousled, robust blond beauty. He reached forward and picked the leaves from her hair with a contented expression.

"Lucky it's not hunting season." He gave her a sly smile.

Sal met his eyes unruffled. "We're in the south, honey. If there were intruders they'd be polite and skedaddle at the sight."

"I suppose you make love in the woods all the time down here?"

Sal shrugged one shapely smooth shoulder.

"I thought southern belles were all proper and nice." Robert ran one finger down her spine.

"Obviously," Sal drawled, "you were wrong."

Robert chuckled as he reached for her sweater and slacks. "Obviously, I was wrong about a lot of things."

"And right about a few." Sal crawled over to him and planted a kiss on his chin. "You wanted to make love that first night in the kitchen."

"I know." He regarded her tenderly. "I was dying for you from the moment I laid eyes on you, Sal. A case of possession."

"And I was dying for you." Sal smiled.

"May it never change." Robert met her eyes solemnly.

"Amen." Sal nodded.

"Now . . ." She stood up and stepped into her underwear as Robert wriggled into his jeans. "When do you have to be back in New York? I'll arrange with Wendell to—"

She felt his hand on her bare waist and turned to him.

"Sal, of course I want you to come to New York. You're right, there are some people I do want you to meet. We'll have a small wedding reception up there.

187

But when I said before that I wanted a change, I meant a change with a capital *C*. I'm going to shut down my New York office, divest myself of a few companies, and putter for a while."

"Putter?" Sal gave him an incredulous smile.

"I'll send you off to New York to grapple with the art world while I stay back here and tend the cows and the kids."

"Kids?"

"Well, I hope." Robert laughed. "At least one of our own and from time to time—"

"Oh, of course—I want us to have room for your kids. What did you mean, putter?"

Robert laughed again, but before he could reply, Sal jumped in with another incredulous question. "You're really going to tend the cows and . . . the child?"

Robert nodded. "I'm going to work on that car battery myself. Maybe what I am at heart is an inventor. Then again, maybe not. But I'll never know till I try. We won't exactly be poor, Sal."

"Oh, I'm not worried about that!" Sal exclaimed. "Only . . . I just bought a house. I mean, I put money down. It's a firm offer, I'd hate to—"

"You want your privacy." Robert narrowed his dark eyes seductively. "I know you. So fix the place up and use it as your creative retreat. We'll fix up our old place and use that as the official manor . . . if that's okay."

"Oh, yes!" Sal felt giddy at the prospects. She slipped the sweater over her head, and after a moment she turned to him hesitantly. There was still one thing.

"What about Abe?" She asked the question reluctantly.

"I feel like a fool about that." Robert met her eyes sheepishly. "I behaved like a neanderthal, right?"

"I'm afraid so," Sal agreed gently.

188

"Well, I'm going to do my damnedest not to," Robert resolved. "Old habits die hard sometimes, Sal. You were right when you said I had an archaic way of looking at men and women. I've never really had a woman as a friend. Not until now, not until you. I never knew it was possible to feel so many things for one woman. Anyway, like I said, I'll do my damnedest where Abe is concerned."

Sal smiled softly. He'd never disappointed her. Once he resolved to do something, once he admitted something needed changing, it was as good as done.

"Once you've fixed your new studio up"—Robert linked his arm through hers as they walked back to where he had dropped his fishing pole—"I think you should offer Abe space there."

"You mean it, don't you?" She nuzzled her chin tenderly on his shoulder.

"Much to my surprise"—Robert's dark eyes darted a fiery glance at her—"I do. There's something about you, Sal, that I will never get over."

All-new **Candlelight Newsletter**

An exceptional, *free* offer awaits readers of Dell's incomparable Candlelight Ecstasy and Supreme Romances.

Subscribe to our all-new CANDLELIGHT NEWSLETTER and you will receive—at absolutely no cost to you—exciting, exclusive information about today's finest romance novels and novelists. You'll be part of a select group to receive sneak previews of upcoming Candlelight Romances, well in advance of publication.

You'll also go behind the scenes to "meet" our Ecstasy and Supreme authors, learning firsthand where they get their ideas and how they made it to the top. News of author appearances and events will be detailed, as well. And contributions from the Candlelight editor will give you the inside scoop on how she makes her decisions about what to publish—and how *you* can try your hand at writing an Ecstasy or Supreme.

You'll find all this and more in Dell's CANDLELIGHT NEWSLETTER. And best of all, *it costs you nothing*. That's right! It's Dell's way of thanking our loyal Candlelight readers and of adding another dimension to your reading enjoyment.

Just fill out the coupon below, return it to us, and look forward to receiving the first of many CANDLELIGHT NEWSLETTERS—overflowing with the kind of excitement that only enhances our romances!

Dell DELL READERS SERVICE—Dept. B500B
P.O. BOX 1000, PINE BROOK, N.J. 07058

Name_____

Address_____

City_____

State_____ Zip_____

Candlelight
Ecstasy Romances™